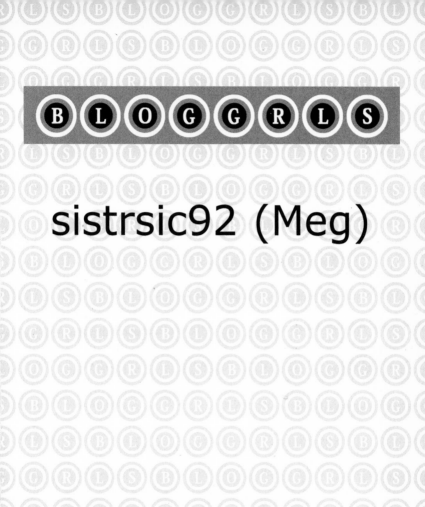

BLOGGRLS

sistrsic92 (Meg)

☹ ♥ ☺

sistrsic92 (Meg)

By Cheryl Dellasega

With illustrations by Tyler Beauford

Marshall Cavendish

Text copyright © 2009 by Cheryl Dellasega
Illustrations copyright © 2009 by Marshall Cavendish Corporation

Marshall Cavendish Corporation
99 White Plains Road
Tarrytown, NY 10591
www.marshallcavendish.us/kids

This book is a work of fiction. Names, characters, places, and incidents are products of the author's imagination
and are used fictitiously. Any resemblance to actual events or locales or persons, living or dead, is entirely
coincidental.

Library of Congress Cataloging-in-Publication Data

Dellasega, Cheryl.
  sistrsic92 (Meg) / by Cheryl Dellasega ; with illustrations by Tyler Beauford. — 1st ed.
     p. cm. — (Bloggrls)
  Summary: As she tries to attract a boyfriend and deal with her beautiful but troubled half-sister, artistically
talented high school sophomore Meg records her thoughts and feelings in a blog—accessible only to her three
closest friends.
  ISBN 978-0-7614-5456-4
  [1. Sisters—Fiction. 2. Anorexia nervosa—Fiction. 3. Eating disorders—Fiction. 4. Interpersonal relations—Fiction.
5. Blogs—Fiction. 6. Youths' art.] I. Beauford, Tyler, ill. II. Title.
  PZ7.D3848Si 2009
  [Fic]—dc22

                          2008053615

Jacket artwork © 2009 by Jane Wattenberg
Book design by Vera Soki
Editor: Marilyn Mark

Printed in China
First edition
10 9 8 7 6 5 4 3 2 1

ɪ̄ɪ̄c Marshall Cavendish

This book is dedicated to all the "Megans" I've known,
who are caught in the middle of a bad situation and trying to survive.
I also want to thank my editor extraordinaire, Marilyn Mark,
whose eye for detail and patient feedback
made this a better book.

 CLICKTIONARY

1: one or won (*as in* 1der, 1derful, every1, *etc*)

2: to, too

4: for (*as in* 4get, b4, 4ever, *etc*)

a10tion: attention

abut: about

afc: away from computer

a/i: as if

altho: although

anthur: another

awesum: awesome

ax: ask

axd: asked

b: be

BBF: Best Boyfriend

b/c: because

bcome: become

bcuz: because

betr: better

BF: Boyfriend

BFF: Best Friend Forever

BGF: Best Girlfriend

bing: being

bk: book

blieve: believe

blong: belong

brb: be right back

brothr: brother

BTDT: Been There Done That

btr: better

btw: by the way

btween: between

c: see

comz: comes

corz: course

craze: crazy

culd: could

culdn't: couldn't

cuz: 'cause

defin8ly: definitely

difrent: different

dint: didn't

doctr: doctor

drivz: drives

dunno: don't know

dunt: don't

duz, duznt: does, doesn't

enuf: enough

eva: ever

evn: even

evry: every

evrythin: everything

eze: easy

famly: family

famus: famous

fav: favorite

fite: fight
frenshipz: friendships
frenz: friends
frm: from
fune: funny
gf: girlfriend, go figure
girlz: girls
goin: going
gr8: great
gr8ly: greatly
gree: agree
grl: girl
grlfrenz: girlfriends
hafta: have to
hansum: handsome
hav: have
heydah: hey there
im: I'm
ima: I'm a
IM'd: instant messaged
imho: in my humble opinion
itz: it's
iz: is
izn't: isn't
kinda: kind of
kno: know
kool: cool
mani: manicure

mebbe: maybe
mite: might
n: and
nd: and
ne: any (as in nething, neway, etc)
neva: never
nite: night
nobode: nobody
norml: normal
nvited: invited
nu: knew, new
nxt: next
OTL: One True Love
OMG: Oh My Gosh
pedi: pedicure
pics: pictures
pitb: pain in the butt
pos: parent over shoulder
ppl: people
pre10d: pretend
problms: problems
prolly: probably
r: are, our
rel8: relate
rnt: aren't
religoz: religious
rents: parents
rilly: really

rite: right
rnt: aren't
romantik: romantic
rote: wrote
sa: say
sed: said
seemd: seemed
sez: says
SF: Sort-of Friend
shud: should
sibs: siblings
sic: sick
sinz: since
sistr: sister
skool: school
sounz: sounds
spcilly: especially
spenz: spends
sukz: sucks
sum: some (*as in* sumday, sumthing, *etc*)
sumtimz: sometimes
tbd: to be determined
tefw: too exciting for words
telz: tells
tgfw: too gross for words
thaz: that's
thnx: thanks

tho: though
thot: thought
thotful: thoughtful
thoz: those
thru: through
tole: told
tolly: totally
tuff: tough
u: you
u'd: you'd
ugle: ugly
u'll: you'll
ur, u r: your, you're
urself: yourself
urselves: yourselves
VBF: Very Best Friend
VBGF: Very Best Girlfriend
V-Day: Valentine's Day
/w: with
w8ting: waiting
wit: with
world fam: world famous
wrekd: wrecked
wtd: what to do
wud: would
wudnt: wouldn't
wut: what
wuz: was

wuzn't: wasn't
x: *substitute for* ex- (*as in* xactly, xciting, *etc*)
y: why
ya: you
z: *substitute for* s (*as in* lotz, boyz, *etc*)

My Profile

General
Name: Meg L.
Birthday: I'm a Gemini—technically
Gender: Female

Interests & Expertise
Interests: Writing, art, reading
Expertise: Working on that—blogger? Doggie daycare provider?
Being second best? (Oh wait—I think I have the last one locked up)
Occupation: Student (boring . . .)

My Buddy List
sistrsic92: that's me!
zo4u: Zoey, from tennis camp
zbest: Lisa, from youth group
tennytrish: Trish, from tennis camp
kyleawhile: Kyle, also from youth group

Thursday, October 1

After five years of creating dozens of cute little pink diaries (okay, one was purple), I've decided to go online and create a blog—and a safe one where my private thoughts won't be spread all over the Internet. I'm pretty sure no one looked at my diaries besides me (what was I thinking in fifth grade when I decided to draw my feelings?), but my sister never missed a chance to give me grief about working on them.

"What's so special in there that you have to keep them under lock and key?" she asked me once, when I slammed the cover shut as she barged into my bedroom. As if she's the only person in our family who's *special*!

Need I say more about why I want privacy?

And guess who is <u>not</u> invited to post on this blog? Unfortunately, pretty much everyone I know since the only people I trust enough to give the password are the three of you.

I hope you give me lots of *congrats* and *chats*—and I'll do the same on your blogs.

Since it's impossible for all of you to meet, let me *introduce* you electronically:

Lisa goes to my church, and although we only see each other on Wednesday nights at youth group and Sundays, she is the kind of person you can tell anything to. She doesn't go to my school, but we sat together on the bus one weekend when we went to a youth retreat, and she told me how she has a perfect older brother and a lot of the same problems I do.

I met **Trish** right after I came to tennis camp and didn't realize how much water you need to drink when you're out there in the sun all day. I was getting lightheaded and shaky, and she came over with a water bottle and gave it to me. She was only at camp for two weeks, but for those two weeks I actually felt like I could become good at tennis (a feeling which would prove to be totally wrong). Trish, however, is a real *ace* at tennis.

Zoey came into my life right after Trish left tennis camp, and I was feeling really lonely. I took one look at her (temporarily) blue hair and knew she'd be fun! Like me she was forced to be there, but at least she has some potential at tennis and tries to play on the team at her school.

(Note: Since I was *forced* to stay at tennis camp all summer it's special that you're the ones I feel closest to. Some of those other campers were downright scary!)

<u>Much</u> more later. . . .
Posted 10/1 @ 11:45 PM

Congrats 6 Chats 3

Hey u! thnx 4 inviting me in. Miss u lotz! <sad sighs from across
the country> Greets to Lisa nd Trish.
Posted 10/2 @ 12:55 AM by zo4u

Back at ya, Zoey. Same here, dear!
Posted 10/2 @ 12:59 AM by zbest

Thnx, heydah!
Posted 10/2 @ 1:00 AM by tennytrish

Friday, October 2

Downstairs, my parents are gaga over my sister Cara's latest
coup—104 on her calculus test. Of course, it isn't enough that
she would get every question right, but all of the extra credit, too.
I've always had a problem with tests where you can get more
than 100%—is that even possible in real life?

Cara is my half sister, and I have a secret name for her: T2P2 (The
Totally Perfect Person). Try saying it out loud and you'll
understand—she's two years older than me, but remember that
word game you played in third grade to find out about opposites?
That would be her and me.

Dellasega

Consider:

Her (Cara)	Yours Truly (The Un-T2P2)
• lots of girl friends	• two sort-of friends, I think
• perfect grades	• average grades
• the most popular guy in the school as her BBF	• never had a real BBF
• just the right height and weight	• too short and a little scrawny
• long, perfectly straight blonde hair	• long brownish hair that always curls but never in the way I want it to
• really blue eyes	• really brown eyes
• flawless skin	• freckles

Now can you see why I have a complex? (Lisa, sorry, I know you've heard this many times before.)

The whole T2P2 thing started one day when I was watching <u>Star Wars</u> for like the 500th time. It occurred to me how cute and helpful and lovable R2D2 was and how my sister is the same, only not in a humorous way but in an annoying, too-good-to-be-true way. It's not that she's mean like the sisters in some of the books I read or in <u>Cinderella</u>, it's just that no one could ever be better than her in any way—especially me.

Add to that the sympathy factor, since her dad died in a tragic car accident right after she was born, and she has an automatic lock on everyone's affection. Is it incredibly small-minded and evil of me to say that? Perhaps—but then I'm not T2P2. I only bring it up because Cara doesn't even remember her biological dad, or the six months she and Mom spent living with Mom's parents and trying to figure out how to make ends meet.

Now those relatives (Mom's) live on the other side of the country, in Washington, and Cara doesn't see them much because they're too old to travel a lot. (They still send her extra cash on her birthdays and Christmas, and sometimes randomly for no reason at all, which is so unfair—I'm related to them, too!)

My dad met my mom while he was in seminary, and they got married when Cara was one and a half. (She says she remembers some of it, but I don't believe that—there are pictures of their wedding everywhere, so even *I* feel like I was there). Not long after, Dad got a "call" to go to a church in Michigan, so they moved there, and I was born a year later. Being a T2P2 (perhaps you have one in your family), Cara never went through the whole sibling rivalry thing—or if she did, she was smart enough to hide it.

Of course, you only have to look at my baby album to appreciate that she didn't have much cause to worry. It was no contest lookswise or personalitywise then, too.

I weighed ten pounds and had a head like a bowling ball, with no hair, and a face constantly screwed up like I was ready to cry. That looked pretty sad next to T2P2 who, even as a toddler, was petite, smiley, and always happy.

The subject of the past doesn't come up often, but sometimes, just sometimes, I think Dad likes me a teeny bit better because we're connected by biology—he has the same sort of bowling-ball head I do, only his isn't covered with a lot of thick brown hair, like mine (thankfully) is now. Still, he's a pastor, so he knows that even if he does prefer me over my sister, you have to hide those things really well.

When I was younger, I tried to impress my parents (okay, I admit it—and everyone else) by striving to be just like T2P2, which was almost not a choice, since teachers would see my last name and get these incredible smiles on their faces—the last ones I would see aimed in my direction.

"Oh my! Are you Cara's little sister?" they would ask on the first day of class, instantly dooming me.

It was always downhill from there. Don't get me wrong: I'm not a bad student or a troublemaker, but I'm not a new improved version of perfection, either. When Dad got another "call" (you really don't want to know how churches do these things; it's sort of like drafting football players with no money, from what I can figure), we moved to upstate New York five years ago. Finally, I thought things might get better, since there would be no T2P2 legacy.

Think again. She seems to get better with age, and before long it was all one big repeat—she was on the honor roll, had a ton of friends, and senior boys were asking her out when she was just a freshman. (Mom and Dad refused to relent on that one, though, even though they admitted T2P2 was *exceptionally mature and responsible.*)

I tried everything to find my own *niche*—debate team (too shy), choir (no talent), craft club (got serious burns with the glue gun), and dog sitting (turns out my own dear doggie is insanely jealous, but we're working on that). In desperation, I decided to try sports, but some girls just aren't meant to play field hockey.

"I can't believe you broke your arm when you ran out on the field to substitute!" T2P2 said when she and Mom came into the ER. I couldn't tell if she was being sneakily sarcastic or really concerned, but the painkiller they gave me probably altered my judgment. The real kicker is that it was midway through the season and my first time on the field. (At my age, T2P2 was a starter.)

That's why, when Mom showed me the brochure for tennis camp last spring, I thought I'd give it a try: it's the one sport T2P2 never had any interest in! (I also discovered it's fairly injury-proof— even when you get hit with a tennis ball you didn't see coming.)

Guess who just invited herself in my room? More later. . . .
Posted 10/2 @ 5:45 PM

Congrats 6 Chats 3

<sound of deep sighs> I shud have such problems . . . my sistrs r so wacked it means I have 2 b the *perfect* 1—not 2 suggest there's nething wrong /w you. . . .
Posted 10/2 @ 6:17 PM by zo4u

Try having a brother who's *perfect*—itz worse, spcilly if ur parents think boyz r always better than girlz.
Posted 10/2 @ 7:10 PM by zbest

2t2c (too tragic to consider). u guyz make me glad im an only child! but at least u have sibs 2 share wut my English teacher calls the "push to be perfect." My mom always wanted 2 b a tennis player nd never culd, so guess who got nominated in her place?
Posted 10/2 @ 8:01 PM by tennytrish

Saturday, October 3

While most girls would be delighted to get their own computer (even if it was a hand-me-down), it was how I got it that made me a little suspicious. My mom, who was probably a lot like T2P2 in her teen years, looked hopefully at my dad and then told me she was upgrading.

"I'm giving you my old computer, Eggy. You like to read so much, maybe you can try writing on your own," she said.

My dad, who never reads into things unless they're religious, hugged me.

"Guess I can count on you for sermon notes from now on?" he said in that jokey voice he uses to make people smile.

(Note: my awful nickname, which comes from the first word I said: egg. Somehow that morphed into Eggy, which sort of fit me as a baby given my huge head and very little hair. Cara's official nickname is "Calla" because she does have one flaw—she couldn't pronounce her name when she was little. But, of course,

<u>calla</u> also happens to be a beautiful flower.)

To be honest, my parents would probably be shocked to read my Cara-bashing, if they could ever find this blog. I picked a site not many people (i.e. T2P2) would look on—did I mention she won a brand-new laptop when she had the highest sales record at CompuCraze, where she worked this summer?

Here she is again.

Maybe all my posts will be rudely interrupted, since some people think their presence is always welcome. . . .
Posted 10/3 @ 8:32 PM

Congrats 2 Chats 1

Try this: put some dental floss across the bottom of ur doorway
where she can't c it (u can wrap it around the door hinge on 1
side nd tack it on the other). Believe me, after 2 *trips,* u won't
b bothered anymore. . . . <sound of maniacal laughter>
Posted 10/3 @ 9:15 PM by zo4u

Monday, October 5

Yesterday being a church day, I didn't get to post, although I did type up some last-minute sermon notes for Dad right before the morning service. I'm an early riser, so I didn't mind—in fact, it made me feel kind of useful.

If you go to church or anything like it where there's a person clearly in charge and it happens to be your dad, you probably know how embarrassing it can be, like you're responsible for everything he says and does. (Lisa knows exactly how it is since her mom is a teacher at her school.) In my case, you also get the label of "PK" (Pastor's Kids), which means everyone thinks you're a Goody Two-shoes and as perfect as Cara really is.

Luckily, Mom doesn't buy into any of that stuff, even when the women in the congregation gossip about her. She lets me and T2P2 wear whatever we want to church and skip services (sometimes) if we feel like it. Every now and then, I hear her and my dad fighting in his study about what Cara and I do and do not have to do in church, but they usually come to an agreement in the end.

There was only one time when she got upset with us (me) for making Dad look bad. That was in kindergarten, when I made a Mother's Day card for her that said, "Thank you for letting Daddy sleep in my room when he snores." Everyone thought it was hilarious but her.

"Megan Marie, remember what your father does for a living," she said as soon as we got home. After that, she made him sleep on the sofa when he got too noisy. (Who knows what people would think about that if they knew.)

Mom works as a real estate agent, which would be a good choice of careers for T2P2 as well. They both have that kind of white-blonde hair that makes everyone stare at them, then pretend not to. They're also the perfect size and shape, just a tiny bit tall and just the right curves in just the right places. As for me . . . when I looked at the self-portrait we had to do in art last year, it could have been an advertisement for *average.*

But hey, even *average* can be interesting—in art class today I got the idea to take a drawing I did and collage around it and then put varnish on top for a kind of distorted effect. My teacher raised his eyebrows when he saw it, and I think he was impressed. At least T2P2 isn't artistic.

Anyway, this summer, before I got packed off to tennis camp, we went to the Jersey Shore for a week, and I saw these two little girls playing in a way only sisters would. The older one kept trying to show the younger one how to build a sand castle, but the younger one (whose name turned out to be Becky) just kept cheerfully dumping sand in her own separate big pile until finally the older one got fed up.

"Leave me 'lone!" Becky yelled and pushed her older sister down. Their mom, who hadn't been watching that closely, only saw the last part and came running over.

"Becky! Be nice to your sister!" she said, brushing sand off the older girl and making sure she was okay.

"BUT SHE HURT MY FEELINGS!" Becky said, and started this fake crying which her mom totally bought into.

"It's okay, honey," she said, forgetting completely about the older sister, who had gotten sand in her eyes and was crying, too, but in a subdued way. The mom gathered Becky up in her arms and made these soothing noises, and in that moment I could see the error of my ways: I've been too accommodating.

When T2P2 suggests I make a sand castle, I do it without complaint, even if I would rather be like Becky and just shovel the biggest hole on the beach. When Becky is my age, I bet she won't let her older sister get any attention, no matter what it takes. That day was when I realized I should have been a different kind of baby.

My friend Jess has four brothers and says they're even worse. "They deliberately mowed over my Barbies—all of them!" she once told me, and that wasn't the worst thing. (The other stuff has to do with bras and underpants, so I won't mention it, should I ever change my mind and let her read my blog—she swore me to secrecy, and that's something I take seriously. That might be my greatest talent—I'm very loyal and a good secret keeper.)

I know blogs are all about your BF and your VBF and so on, but I never see anyone write about an SF—which is what Jess is. I actually have a lot of *sort-of* friends, but she's the one I've known longest. Why are we just *sort-of* and not *best* or *very best* friends? When you're really quiet like I am, you kind of don't know what the other person is feeling, so you're never sure of your status. (That's why I love having blog buds like you guys!)

Anyway, me and Jess have known each other ever since I moved here in 5th grade, and she tells me some personal stuff (like above), but last year, in the middle of the year, she invited Maritza, a new girl, to sit at our lunch table. (Maybe I should say that Maritza, who is definitely *outspoken,* invited herself, and Jess didn't object.)

Since she started eating lunch with us, Maritza has become, by default, another *sort-of* friend, but now I'm reevaluating even that. Last week I found out that Jess invited Maritza on her birthday trip to New York City! They went to see a play and spend the night in a hotel with Jess's mom. Jess told me it was because last year she took me to Hershey Park for her birthday trip, which is true, but it still made me feel really bad.
Posted 10/5 @ 5:02 PM

Congrats 2 Chats 3

<murmurs of sympathy> I kno xactly how u feel—my former VBF tolly ditched me nd nvited anthur grl 2 San Fran 4 a weekend. They made sure I nu about it, of course, so we r no longer VBF or BF or even SF. I hang out wit mostly guyz as I told u at camp bcuz they r so much nicer than grlz.
Posted 10/5 @ 6:19 PM by zo4u

R u kidding? Guyz r worse than grlz, they dunt even care how they look or if they take a shower, which iz tgfw. I tried having a guy as a friend, but he ended up thinking I liked him—in that BBF way! So much 4 him. Then there's my older brothr who iz just evil xcept my parents dont c it. Jess nd I culd tolly rel8 abut that.
Posted 10/5 @ 7:30 PM by zbest

Meg, that is so sad, like a movie or sumthing where girlz r mean 2 each other. Jess shud have told her mom she wanted u 2 come 2. After all, Maritza wuzn't around when u went to Hershey! (izn't that place great? My parents took me when I wuz little nd I still remember it!)
Posted 10/5 @ 8:00 PM by tennytrish

Tuesday, October 6

Last night, I was walking by the front door when I noticed that Trip, T2P2's BBF and the school's star basketball player, was bringing her home from the game. (To be honest, when I heard the car door slam, I started spying out the living room window, which you can easily do if you separate the curtains a little bit.)

When she started to come in the house, he grabbed her and kissed her really hard, right there on the front porch with all the lights on! At first she tried to push him away, but then she stepped into some shadows, and they kept making out about five feet in front of me. I've seen them kissing lots of times before, and I was about ready to barf and then leave (or vice versa), but before I could, Trip put his hand right up under her sweater. Of course, T2P2 slapped it away, but this morning at breakfast, Mom came in the kitchen while we were eating breakfast and her cheeks were really red like they get when she's mad. "Were you and Trip kissing on the front porch last night?" she asked T2P2, who innocently kept eating her toast.

"Mom, it was just a kiss, it was nothing," she said, dabbing crumbs away from her mouth with a napkin and standing up. "Why, was Mrs. Baptiste on the lookout again?"

Mrs. Baptiste, aka Mrs. B, is our ancient neighbor who has no life other than spying. She goes to our church, so Dad is a bit of a celebrity to her, even if she loves to criticize him: our house needs painting, our dog Casper peed in her yard, my mom's skirt was too short, and so on. It's sort of sad, really, since no one ever comes to visit her. When Casper runs into her yard and I have to chase him, she always traps me into really long conversations where she does most of the talking. (And she grew up in France, so when she gets going it's hard to figure out what she says, and when she calls me *chérie* I don't believe for a minute she really means it.)

Dad never gets upset with Mrs. B, but Mom sure does. When Dad took over some Christmas cookies last year, he had to do it alone because Mom said it would be hypocritical of her to go, and that she might say something they both would regret.

Of course, Mom totally believed T2P2's explanation about Trip, and the red went out of her cheeks. Only I knew that when Trip got his hand slapped, he just laughed and shoved it back up my sister's sweater, trying again and again until she gave up and let him do it.
Posted 10/6 @ 4:01 PM

Congrats o Chats o

Friday, October 9

Today, Jess told me I should be a librarian when I grow up. She came home with me after school and took a look around my room and said, "Eggs, you need to find something besides books to spend your time on." (Note, however, that perhaps she is more than an SF, because she does use my special nickname, abbreviated. But then again, she's only invited me over to her house five times since school started, and one doesn't really count because it was a sleepover with four other girls, including Maritza.)

SF or BF—You Be the Judge

• Jess eats lunch with me every day, but she only talks to me like a friend when we're alone.

• We both like to draw and carry our sketch pads everywhere, but Jess likes to listen to music on her iPod while she works, and I don't. That means it's mostly silent when we draw together.

• She comes from a rich family—her parents buy her everything she wants. I come from a kind of rich family, but my dad believes in *living modestly* (there's a surprise).

• She babysits every Friday night, while I have *issues* with little kids. (Okay, so I'm the only person who let a kid escape from the church nursery—how was I to know the little guy was headed for his parents instead of the bathroom? Dad told me it was pretty funny when he burst in the church and said "Mommy!" at the top of his lungs, but he also said maybe childcare was not a good option for me.)

• She wants to be *popular* just like Maritza. They always try and horn in on the cheerleader clique at lunch, since they sit right next to us, but those girls scare me—being happy to have someone throw you up in the air is just not normal. I admit I may feel that way because I tried out last year and couldn't get up after I did the split. Everyone laughed, and I felt like Casper must when we yell at him for getting into the garbage.

• Jess is cute (red hair, green eyes, and the kind of freckles that look good, unlike mine) and has two boys who like her, while I am . . . well, I think she'd agree that my self portrait was pretty accurate.

Maritza is another matter. She is so not eligible for the BF category, because I know she feels jealous that I've known Jess longer than she has, and she tries to suck up all the time. She also makes fun of me right to my face but pretends it's just a joke. Here are some of her recent takebacks:

"Meg, where did you find that shirt? It looks so Goodwill."
"Wow, <u>somebody</u> forgot to comb her hair this morning."
"I would never eat white bread. It's like pure chemicals, and we all know what that does to your brain."

After each one of these, she smiles and pretends like it's funny, but it isn't.

On the plus side, Maritza <u>can</u> be pretty funny, especially when she speaks Spanish, which neither Jess or I really understand (three years of school Spanish is just not the same as living in a family that speaks it every day). And Maritza is a fantastic photographer, too. Maybe that's what ties the three of us together, since we each have some kind of artistic ability and are in the honors art class, but Maritza is clearly the best (and lets us know it). She's been telling us she's sure Mr. Walker will pick her to be in AAP, the Academic Arts Program for really good art students, but Cara told me sophomores rarely get selected. (I didn't want Maritza to turn on me, so to speak, so I kept that information to myself.)

As Dad said in one of his sermons, I try to take the good <u>and</u> the bad.
Posted 10/9 @ 3:34 PM

Congrats 2 Chats 3

Weird, one of my new (nd only girl) BFs is Hispanic 2, I guess u call them Latina when itz a girl which sounds sort of cool, imho. Get urslf invited 2 her house bcuz their food is 2 die 4. My BF's dad roasted a pig which soundz 2 gross if u r an animal rites person, but it was so good I ate until I thot I wud barf! <sounds of moaning but happiness>
Posted 10/9 @ 6:10 PM by zo4u

Itz sorta like that 4 me, 2, since my VBFs r on the tennis team /w me nd sumtimes they leave me out of thingz. My mom sez three girlz never workz out.
Posted 10/9 @ 7:00 PM by tennytrish

I hafta tell u when Jess came to church /w u that 1 time I thot she seemd a little stuck up, I mean mebbe itz high standards, like she wudnt be friends /w just anyone. but u r so funny in ur own way nd thotful—remember when u drew that pic 4 me 2 cheer me up after my BBF dumped me? dunno—mebbe u rnt meant 2 b frenz wit her?
Posted 10/9 @ 9:06 PM by zbest

Tuesday, October 20
Here I sit, surrounded by books. Jess is right, I have them piled everywhere in my room so that not even Mom, a Martha Stewart

21

clone, can organize it. Sometimes I try to downsize, and Dad'll take me to the Swap Shop on Saturday mornings with a bunch of donations, but I usually end up bringing back a bagful of extras.

"Isn't the idea to clear some space in your room?" he'll ask when we drive home, his eyebrows just a little lifted so I know he secretly thinks it's kind of funny—not to mention he has a bag of his own in the trunk.

"They're not all for me," I protest, which is true. I do give Jess and Maritza the ones about art that I think they'll like, and Lisa, you get the sci-fi/fantasy ones, but even someone as ungifted as I am at algebra knows that what's going off my bookshelves is less than what's going back on.

Our school library is the nicest place in the building, with four big skylights in the ceiling, so it's sort of like heaven right above you. The librarian has a reputation like most do, but she's actually really cool if she knows you love books. At the beginning of the month, she always lets me sit in her office to eat lunch so I can be the first to look through the new issues of my favorite magazines. This is where my theory of *sort-of friends* comes in—Jess and Maritza never even ask me where I've been when I'm not there on those days.

I'm not around seniors much, but today I had to take a shortcut through *their* hallway because I left my homework in my locker. It's like entering a big, dark forest because most of them are way taller than I am and kind of threatening.

I was trying to hurry through, when who should I see with a bunch of his friends but Trip. Before I could get past him, he stopped listening to what his friends were saying and came over to block my way.

"Hey, little sister," he said, messing my hair like he does every time he sees me. (He rubs Casper's head in exactly the same way.)

His friends all started laughing, and I'm sure my face got as red as Mom's did when she confronted Cara about the kissing. I kept walking, but couldn't help hearing Trip say my sister's name, then something else that made his friends hoot.

I felt like such a dork it actually made me cry after school when I was safe in my bedroom and thought about it. In some twisted way I felt loyal to T2P2 and didn't want her to get hurt by a stupid boy. Wouldn't you know, she walked in my room right when I blew my nose for the tenth time and bugged me until I told her what happened.

Usually when I'm emotional, she'll say something like, "Don't worry about that," or "Eggy, get a grip," but this time she just sat down next to me on my bed and put one arm around my shoulders.

It was quiet until Casper trotted in the room and wormed his way between us. I wondered what she was thinking, but before I could ask, Mom called us downstairs for supper, and when Trip called later on, Cara acted like absolutely nothing was wrong.
Posted 10/20 @ 9:35 PM

Congrats 2 Chats 1

<sounds of grrrrr> No grl shud eva let a boy make her cry!!!! Nxt time u c Trip u shud pre1od 2 drop ur heaviest bk rite on his foot ☺
Posted 10/20 @ 9:46 PM by zo4u

Monday, October 26

Like most girls my age (or at least the few I actually talk to), I would love to have a boyfriend, although if he was like Trip (and most of the boys at our school are that immature), I'm not sure it would be worth it. My little romance at tennis camp this past summer was the closest I've ever come to having a BBF, and now I haven't heard from him since we said good-bye. 🙁

This all happened after you left, Trish, so I'm not sure how much you know. Here's what happened (Zoey, add details as appropriate, and Lisa, sorry to tell this story ONE MORE TIME!).

It all started when I got assigned to be partners with the best player at camp. Poor Mark! I thought he was going to throw his racket when the coach called out my name.

"Who knows? Maybe Megan's a doubles player," coach said, not adding the obvious—I clearly wasn't a singles player.

Until that point, judging from the way most of the kids acted when they got paired to play singles with me, I was on target to get the unofficial award as biggest loser at the closing ceremony. (Of course, I made everyone feel great about their own ability because they always beat me by a lot, even the ones who weren't very good. At least Zoey and I had a good time when we played together, right? Who knew you could lose a whole can of tennis balls in one morning?)

After his initial surprise, Mark was different—really nice and encouraging. (He's a junior in high school and a superjock—good at a lot of sports, but especially tennis.) When he found out I didn't play tennis year round and had been forced to come to camp for a whole summer because it was my mom's busy selling season and my sister was working just about every day, he got a look in his eyes like the angels in the stained-glass window that got donated to the church.

(Aside—Dad wanted me to go to Camp Ne-wak-a, the church camp I've gone to every other summer and tolerated, but Mom said it was time for something different. Even though it's a church camp, no one at Camp Ne-wak-a ever looked or acted like an angel, so I took Mark's reaction as a good sign.)

Trish and Zoey know that camp was *closely supervised,* and my counselor (April) was on a real power trip, so she watched us like a hawk—to be honest, I think she was a little jealous that any of us would attract a boy. (Trish, you are soooo lucky you were in another cabin. Zoey, remember when you snuck out that night to meet you-know-who, and she came after you and reported you to the camp director?)

Anyway, Mark asked if we could keep on being partners, which at first made me suspicious, because who would want to guarantee himself a sure loss? But when he was so nice, I tried really hard to be good at tennis, and we actually tied one game.

I won't go into the details of what happened on the last day of camp, but suffice it to say we *eluded* April for an hour, and I won't ever claim to be *sweet sixteen and never kissed.* I've emailed him three times (he hasn't answered), but I haven't completely lost hope. He promised he would stay in touch!
Posted 10/26 @ 7:30 PM

Congrats 6 Chats 3

Awww u r still sweet!
Posted 10/26 @ 7:48 PM by zbest

I kno who u r talking abut. Evry1 had a crush on him—u dint say how cute he iz wit dimples nd blue eyes that do look angelic, nd lots of curly black hair! Plus evn tho he is clearly going 2 bcome famous sumday, he wuz nice, unlike sum others who thot they were on their way to Wimbleton. (even *sum* counselors culd b that way—like April!)
Posted 10/26 @ 8:05 PM by tennytrish

How roMANtik! <soundz of being overcome by emotion> but rilly, 4 an *elite* tennis camp, that place wuz the pitz, dunt u think? My rents made me go, 2, but thaz been evry summer sinz 6th grade, when they thot I mite be good enuf 2 get a scholarship or play pro. (u saw how bad I am!) Itz so hard at my school since tennis is a tolly prep sport nd I am a tolly unprep person, nd bcuz in California u have 2 play year round!

But I decided 2 quit bcuz the other girls made fun of me for wearing only black to practice (as if it's ne hardship to them!) Yesterday while I wuz in the shower they put pink paint all over my stuff, nd when my mom called the school 2 complain, nothing happened. (surprised? Wut was she thinking?)

neway, as I told u, I have guy frenz now nd there is a big drama bcuz 2 of them want me to go out /w them: 1 is a game geek nd spenz more time wit his computer screen than me, but he is very cute, while the other is just a techno-machine geek, who likes 2 take things apart nd figure out how they work nd is trying 2 teach me abut car engines. <fluttering of eyelids> oh, 2 be so adored!
Posted 10/26 @ 8:19 PM by zo4u

Monday, November 2

T2P2 has started jogging with Dad in the morning, even though it's wicked cold out and she is much slower than him. She's already the star of swim team and really good at field hockey, so I think this is just a secret way to suck up. Still, he was happy she wanted to spend time with him, since I heard him tell Mom her relationship with Trip is getting too *serious*. If he only knew!

It's supposed to snow tonight! I'm so excited since that means school might be cancelled and then Mom will stay home and watch reruns with us. This is kind of a slow time of year for her at work, which gives her the opportunity to pay more attention than usual to our lives. (This can be both good and bad.) But if it's a really big snow, maybe Dad will go tobogganing with me, which Cara thinks is so *juvenile* but which he and I love. (Zoey, you haven't lived until you've flown down a hill at like 40 miles an hour on a piece of wood!)

Mom is always busy, though. She sent for a lot of college catalogs for T2P2 since she's a senior and keeps mentioning that she's going to schedule me for a "makeover" at the place where she gets her hair cut. She also spends a lot of time making up the "Welcome!" baskets she gives all her customers so they are all over the house— except for Dad's study because she knows it's off limits.

"Watch and learn, Eggy," Mom tells me, which means I have to help her put soup mix and maps of our town into dozens of wicker baskets she orders online at a discount. "Someday when you're in the business world, you'll see how it's the little things like this that make you successful."

She is successful—last year she got named to something called the Five Million Dollar Club, which means she sold a lot of *properties.* It's not hard to imagine her with a big smile and one of those welcome baskets in her hand, all cheerleaderish about the houses she wants to sell, even if they're *fixer-uppers* (real estate speak for total dumps).

Our house would fall into that category, since we live in this super- old place right next to the church, where Dad says we have to stay, even if the plumbing does back up and the fuse box overloads at least once a month. That doesn't stop Mom from dragging him around to look at new houses in big developments, where you don't have Mrs. B types as your too-close-for-comfort neighbors.

"It's a good investment, and just because you're a minister doesn't mean you shouldn't live in a nice house," Mom says when he (inevitably) tells her, "I don't think so" every time they go out for a *preview.*

If it wouldn't hurt his feelings, I'd tell Dad I wish we could move, too. (Preferably next door to Lisa!) Jess and Maritza live about five miles apart, so they can go over to each other's houses all the time, but there's only one kid from my school who lives in our neighborhood, and she's T2P2's VBF Tonya, so you can imagine my chances of hanging out with her. One time they did let me come in her room while they were trying on clothes. After they convinced me to let them put a (barely noticeable) red streak in my hair, and Mom flipped out at me, I figured it wasn't worth it.
Posted 11/2 @ 5:10 PM

Congrats 2 Chats 3

Hey my hair is blue nd red stripes right now (see pic on my blog) nd no one even comments. <feelings of slight disappointment nd consideration of more extreme measures? A third stripe?> thatz the norm here. My dad is "in the industry" but then who isn't in L.A.? <insert finger in throat> I used to think he was a drag but a pastor pop mite be worse.

Victory! Zeb (computer geek) has won the battle for my ♥ <sounds of extreme pitter patter!> Unfortunately, it has ruined our frenshipz /w the rest of our crowd since thingz got a little ugle nd even physical between him nd Mack (engine guy) b4 I made up my mind. Of corz, evry1 at skool sez ima slut bcuz they both liked me—a/i! im prolly the only grl in my skool who hasn't done it yet, which is why I like Zeb—hez not pushy that way.
Posted 11/2 @ 6:03 PM by zo4u

The big thing at my skool rite now is having a white stripe down the middle of your dark hair, or vice versa. It culd either be a very cool Morticia kind of thing, or a tolly uncool skunk look, depending on the kid.

Hey Zoey, I can't believe we both live in California, even if you're like five hours away from me. 2 bad I left camp so soon nd dint get 2 kno u.
Posted 11/2 @ 9:10 PM by tennytrish

Zoey, you goey. Get that guy and make him yours, just like they do in books—if you need ideas I can mail you some of my favorites! I used some of the flirt-but-pretend-you're-not techniques I read about on Mark!
Posted 11/2 @ 10:00 PM by sistrsic92

Thursday, November 5

Pastor pop—I like that, and even he thought it was kind of funny when I told him. Although Jess has always thought it's weird to have a dad who's a pastor and puts on her very best behavior whenever she's around him, there are some good things about his job. Like we get lots of cookies at Christmastime and funny presents on Dad's birthday, plus Mrs. B isn't the only one who treats him (and me and T2P2, to a lesser extent) like a celebrity. The congregation knows when our birthdays are, and that I have a dog named Casper, and a whole bunch of other details about our lives, including the story of Cara's dad.

Most of the older women in our congregation think Dad is wonderful, which is important in any church (if they don't like you, you get put in that big pool of pastors waiting for a "call" and hope for the best). Sometimes, they scold Mom for not taking good enough care of him or us. (Usually she just laughs and pretends it's a joke and tells them they can come over and cook dinner any time, but I suspect that's because some day, many of them will have houses to sell. . . .)

Speaking of T2P2, tonight at supper Mom actually yelled at her: "You hardly ate anything! You're on the swim team and now you're running—a salad just doesn't cut it, Cara."

"Coach says we should eliminate fat from our diet," T2P2 said, pushing her plate away. (For a second I considered grabbing it because Mom's barbecued chicken is too good to go to waste. Plus, I'm sick of hearing Cara's latest obsession: a running calculation of the fat content in every bite she eats.)

Mom pushed the plate right back at T2P2 and said she couldn't get up from the table until she ate more. For the first time I witnessed a real battle between the two of them, which is majorly significant in my house. Dad happened to be at a meeting (when isn't he?), so the two of them screamed at each other <u>forever</u> and then—prepare yourself—T2P2 picked up her plate and threw it against the wall!

I won't go into why Mom uses the dishes Great Grandma Bess gave her for everyday meals, but that happened to be the plate the chicken was on. When it shattered all over the floor, there was this moment like in the movies where two people with guns are facing each other, ready to shoot. Who would pull the trigger first?

The normal T2P2 would never throw a bone china plate with a gold rim—but if she did, she would have been beside herself with apologies and helped Mom clean up the mess. What am I saying? T2P2 would offer to get an extra job to replace the entire set of dishes and repaint the "Parchment White" wall Mom and Dad spent weekends this past summer working on.

But not this time—in fact, it seemed like someone totally different was living in my sister's skin. That someone lifted her chin as if to say, "So there!" and marched upstairs to her room, slamming the door loud enough to make sure we heard it.

Mom looked at me and said, "Eggy, what just happened?" The confident real estate expression was wiped right off her face.

Why would she think I might have an explanation for something so weird? All I could do was to go over and start picking up the plate that was now laying in about eight pie-shaped pieces on the floor. Suddenly I wasn't very hungry, either.

Posted 11/5 @ 9:32 PM

Congrats 2 Chats 2

Gf. While I am the most reasonable woman in my family <shoulders back nd head up, bowing 2 applause,> my oldest older sister is wacko /w a capital W. She's been in nd out of rehab so many times she knows all these movie stars who got in trouble nd were court ordered 2 go 2. When I think abut the future I see urs truly as a fabulously successful fashion designer wit homes in Róme nd New York City nd her going 2 the nursing home to scream at my parents because they won't give her more money. The verdict on the in-betweener is still out. . . .

Posted 11/5 @ 9:45 PM by zo4u

Wow, that is rilly weird—do u think itz a delayed reaction to neva

getting 2 kno her biological dad? Im taking psychology this
semester, nd itz incredible wut can happen if u get screwed up
over ur parents.
Posted 11/5 @ 10:07 PM by tennytrish

Tuesday, November 10

Cara—I can no longer call her T2P2—is a mess. Mom and Dad
have to bug her every night about eating, which is so strange
because I was in her room this morning looking for my favorite
white blouse that she often *borrows* without even asking and
found all these boxes of junk food in her closet under piles of
clothes. You know the stuff I'm talking about—pure sugar.
Seriously, she could have opened her own convenience store.

If I had swim practice twice a day and ran with Dad every morning,
I would be ravenous. (I ate about 4,000 calories a day when I was
at tennis camp, even if my nickname was *Lead Butt*.) Maybe
that's the reason for the snack store in her closet—but I can't tell
Mom to stop worrying about her getting enough calories, because
I'll get completely trashed for being a snitch and a snoop. I've
started to eat in front of the TV just to avoid it all.

Enough about her—I do finally have some *news* to share. Guess
who has been asked to be part of the Academic Arts Program
(AAP)? Me! It's so amazing, overwhelming, and unexpected, I keep
thinking Mr. Walker will tell me tomorrow in homeroom that he
made a mistake. This is a serious national contest, unlike the
ones in the newspaper where anyone can draw a picture of a tree
and send it in—so why was I picked?

"Your art teacher gave me recommendations," he said, sneaking a glance at the list in his hand again when I asked that question. Maybe he wondered if he misunderstood and the names on there were ones he definitely should <u>not</u> ask. . . .

It must be true, though, because he gave me a bunch of forms about the program, which starts next week, and told me I will have to stay after school at least two afternoons a week and start going around to different art exhibits (unless you count the religious art Dad has taken us to see in museums, I've never been to one) with him and the other *candidates*. There's also this big art competition at the end of the year—I'm so excited! I have to get Mom and Dad's permission, though, which might be easy or hard, given their current level of obsession with Cara's caloric intake.

Another downer: Maritza got asked but Jess didn't. We were the only sophomores chosen, so it was hard not to be extra excited, but I felt so bad when I came in the bathroom and found Jess crying. . . . I told her she's a really good artist, so maybe they just missed her—she should definitely ask Mr. Walker about it, I think.
Posted 11/10 @ 7:17 PM

Congrats 4 Chats 2

<cheering nd high fives> Wow! Evry1 here thinks they have *artistic talent* but of course none of them do, just famous dads or moms who get them opportunities no 1 else wud have. Last year my dad got me a gig singing background for a commercial, nd it turned out a little like ur field hockey experience. They never told me I had to learn the music by heart b4 it was taped! Sumtimes adults r so clueless.

I am so anti-school this year I don't spend a minute more there than I have 2, xpecially since I quit tennis. Of course, my parents think Im still on the team nd all these clubs, but itz just an excuse to go 2 Zeb's house nd hang out. . . . ☺ Like they wud notice neway. They actually think my sister the addict has a chance of getting in 2 college nd keep taking her around 2 look at different places. Did I tell u when we were IMing that I caught her taking fifty dollars out of my mom's purse? she acted like there was nothing wrong /w it!
Posted 11/10 @ 9:10 PM by zo4u

Eggs—u need more confidence in urself! Of course it wuznt a mistake to ask u 2 b in the art program, nd imho, u r prolly better than Jess bcuz u work rilly hard at everything u do!
Posted 11/10 @ 10:00 PM by zbest

Thursday, November 12

Zoey, I can't believe our lives are so alike!

Today I was in the cafeteria, and although I know I am never allowed to speak to my sister at school unless she initiates the conversation, I do look for her from time to time. (It's not hard—find the loudest, most crowded table, and she's in the center.) So I couldn't help noticing her sitting there eating a salad one tiny bite of lettuce at a time. How weird is that? Of course, Trip had his hands all over her, or at least as much as he can on school property, but she kept swatting him away like a fly.

It gets stranger. When I was going to study hall, Cara's VBF Tonya (the one from our neighborhood) stopped me in the hallway.

"What's up with your sister?" she asked, like I know everything that goes on in anyone's life!

"In regard to?" I asked back. (Nicely done, I think.)

"Duh." Tonya gave me this haughty look and shook her head like it had been a huge mistake to ask me anything at all. "She doesn't eat anymore, in case you hadn't noticed."

I wanted to snap back, "You think?" in my most sarcastic voice, but by the time I thought of it, she was gone.

This is my life: Cara, Cara, Cara. I'm sick of her, and more so now that she's found a way to get <u>even more</u> attention for herself.

Dad signed the permission form last night, so I'm officially part of the AAP! There were some uncomfortable moments at the lunch table today when Maritza started telling me all this stuff about AAP that she looked up online. I'm pretty sure Jess was crying in the bathroom again, because we have English together right after lunch and her eyes were all puffy—plus, she wouldn't talk to me when class was over. If I had to pick between being in AAP with her or Maritza, I would choose her any day, but of course I can never tell her that.

Anyway, she doesn't have to worry about me and Maritza becoming best friends or anything, since it's not Maritza's style to associate exclusively with someone as unpopular as me—Jess is like that buffer person who makes it okay.

A lot of older girls are nice to Jess because of her brothers, and sometimes they invite her to do something with them in the hopes they will meet one of her brothers and snag a boyfriend, but they are in for a surprise. Jess describes her brothers as *uniquely weird,* and I have to admit, I would have to be desperate before I dated one of them, even if they are cute like her. (Clearly this goes against popular opinion.)

Anyway, back to AAP. Everyone has to make a portfolio of artwork and write about it, so Mr. Walker will be spending lots of time with us. So far, all I know about him is that he's the typical home-room teacher, all official and business and disciplinarian. He wears a wig, I'm pretty sure. Someone told me it's because his hair is really long and the school hassles him about it, but that can't be worse than a retro plastic haircut!
Posted 11/12 @ 6:45 PM

Congrats 2 Chats 1

At my school, you can't tell the teachers from sum of the students. Parents complain abut it all the time, xpesh when there's some big exposé of a teacher dating one of his or her students. But wut can you xpect, rilly? Like Peter Pan (my fav movie, I confess), sooner or later you have 2 act like a grown-up, even when you don't want 2. My VBF's mom is that way—she buys her clothes in a store for teenagers! I wud die of embarrassment.

Neway, do the guyz in the art program have potential? You can't wait for Mark forever, u kno. Or has he emailed back? Hope so!
Posted 11/12 @ 11:34 PM by tennytrish

Tuesday, November 17

No word from Mark, and unfortunately, the artistically inclined guys in our school are probably that way because art is all that matters to them. There are seven guys in the group, and none of them has ever been seen with a girl, according to Maritza.

The one I think is cutest is this senior, Jeremy, who's no Mark, but who is wicked good at drawing. When I was describing the other kids in the program to Mom and Dad at supper, Cara piped up and said the rumor is Jeremy is gay, because he's only interested in art and has a *gay guy* name.

"Cara," Dad said, frowning at her. (Even he is beginning to lose patience with her.) "I'm surprised to hear you make a judgment like that."

I'm not—that kind of mean comment is so typical of her lately. Tonya must have somehow irritated her (or vice versa), because they haven't been hanging out lately, and yesterday, after Mrs. B made another comment to Dad about *public shows of necking,* she took a disposable camera over to Mrs. B's house!

"Next time when you spy on me and my boyfriend, you can take a picture," Cara apparently told her. You can imagine Dad had to do some fast talking to smooth that one over.

I've already started playing around with some drawing stuff, which I'll bring to church on Sunday so at least Lisa can see it. Trish and Zoey, maybe I can put some of it online. I'm really liking the collage piece I'm working on. I added in some little pieces of fabric and snippets from books I've read (although part of me feels like I'm chopping up a friend!), and it has potential. Mr. Walker says he thinks I should keep focusing on *mixed media* which describes me perfectly.

Posted 11/17 @ 12:45 PM

Congrats 2 Chats 0

Wednesday, November 18

So I don't have a lot of time to write, but here's a quick update: AAP totally rocks—it feels like a place where I can really be me— or at least as much as I can be around Maritza. It's interesting to have it be just me and her, though, since there are things I really like about Maritza, like her wicked sense of humor. But if I want to be in the shadow of someone's limelight, I can do that at home with T2P2.

I admit I am *interested* in Jeremy. Here are the few things I've

been able to figure out about him:
• He has really nice hands and clean fingernails (unless a guy is a car guy like Zoey's almost-boyfriend, grubbiness is a turnoff)
• His drawing is incredibly detailed—he spends forever on the smallest thing, like the leaf on a tree
• Most of his wardrobe is comfy clothes like T-shirts and jeans that have been washed enough so they're soft and slouchy
• He has naturally curly brown hair and thoughtful eyes

Not bad. Here's a sketch of what he looks like:

Posted 11/18 @ 3:48 PM

Congrats 4 Chats 3

HEYDAH! I thot u sed he wuznt cute!
Posted 11/18 @ 4:31 PM by tennytrish

Either ur a very good artist (true) or he is a modern day Romeo
(reading R & J in English class rite now. . . .) Bring him 2 church!
Posted 11/18 @ 5:15 PM by zbest

wut a cutie <sounds of heart beating faster from a long distance>
Go 4 it!
Posted 11/18 @ 10:28 PM by zo4u

Friday, November 27

Yummy. . . . I love everything about Thanksgiving, not just the
food but the smells and the excitement and the time off from
school, of course. My grams flew in from Florida, and Dad's
brother and his family drove all the way from Wisconsin. That
made it ten people squashed into a house normally meant for
four. My three cousins are okay but a lot younger than me, so all
they wanted to do was play video games, which I'm so beyond.

Although Grams is always proud of Dad for being a pastor, his
brother, Alex, isn't. My gramps was a pastor, too, so maybe Uncle
Alex is stuck with his own version of the perfect sibling, but he's
nice enough to me. (It's possible by the time I get to be as old as
him, I'll feel the same way about Cara.) His wife, Gina, is your
basic aunt, obliged to ask how school is going and then move on
to drink wine in the kitchen with Mom.

So why do I like all this so much? I guess in contrast to the normal do-your-own-thing days, it's one time when everyone dedicates themselves (or tries) to being happy. It snowed a lot this afternoon, so we all went out tobogganing, which was really fun. Scratch that: Aunt Gina, Mom, and Grams stayed at the house and cleaned up the massive mess from dinner, while the rest of us bundled up and drove to this killer hill not far from our house. (I can't sit comfortably because of the bruise on my butt from a major wipeout I had!)

Cara seemed like her old self, even though I did notice she kind of pushed the food around on her plate at dinner so she wouldn't have to eat a lot of it. Mom was too busy with other things to bug her. Cara won at all the board games we played and then let Ella, our six-year-old cousin, brush her hair while we all watched a movie. Despite my *challenges* with child care, Ella is a cutie, especially when she decided to *help* me arrange my books in order from shortest to tallest.

"That way your room will be all nice and neat, cousin Eggy," she said. But after one shelf, she got distracted by Casper, who delights in attacking piles of books and knocking them over.

For Christmas we have to fly out to Washington to see Mom's family, which makes me sad already, because I'll have to leave my little snow bunny Casper behind. ☹ ☹ ☹ Plus, it's just not fun to be away from home for Christmas, but that's the deal.
Posted 11/27 @ 8:56 AM

Congrats 2 Chats 1

Heydah. Can u believe it, my rents have six brothers n sisters

btween them so itz like an invasion here on holidays. U r a betr
sport than me—I hate sharing my room nd having 2 b nice
all the time to my snotty cousins, spcilly when im used 2 ruling
the roost!

Posted 11/27 @ 10:04 AM by tennytrish

Monday, November 30

Mrs. B waved me down today when I was coming home from
school with my portfolio under one arm.

"So you're an artist, are you?" she asked me.

I mumbled something about AAP, and she insisted I come in her
house and show her my drawings. Have I said how much I hate
her house? It's always too hot and has this old-person smell, like
too much dust in the air or something. Dad says we should be
nice to her, though, so I went in.

At first I just showed her a couple of my older drawings, but then
she reached right into my portfolio and pulled out the piece I was
working on with the fabric and the book parts. She took a sharp
breath in.

"*Magnifique!* Megan, did you do this?" She put the gold glasses
she wears on a chain around her neck on the bridge of her nose
and looked at my drawing for a long time, tilting the paper one
way and then the other. "Very clever." She handed it back to me
and made a gesture with her hand. "Come on, let me see the rest."

I laid the three pieces I've been playing with lately on her dining-
room table, which had this ancient lace tablecloth on it. (They

45

looked kind of nice there, so I made a mental note to try collaging lace over my next drawing.) After Mrs. B studied each one of them, she said she'd be right back and hobbled off into another room. She wasn't *right back,* but when she came out she had these three oil paintings that were really good, if you like paintings.

"I did these when I was living in <u>Paris</u>," she told me, laying them on the table so I could take a closer look. To be polite, I acted really interested in them, but it actually wasn't that hard, since she could easily get her work in a museum (turns out she has!).

"Sometime, I'll get out all the slides of my paintings and we can look at them together," she said as I managed to end the conversation and ease out the door.

In your dreams, I thought, and instantly realized how very bad this must sound to God.

"That would be fun," I sort of choked out, then wondered if it is worse to lie or be sarcastic. Still, she might be a negative old woman, but even I have to admit she's a wicked good artist.
Posted 11/30 @ 7:59 PM

Congrats 4 Chats 2

Im not religoz, but I think u were nice 2 her. (my rents tell me 2 do the same w/ old ppl.) Nd who knoz, mebbe in 2025 u will look at her slides again <sounds of many hehes> oh I just realized thaz so not funny bcuz she prolly won't b around.
Posted 11/30 @ 9:10 PM by zo4u

U hafta kno Eggy's dad—he is way cool nd makes religion kinda fun nd interesting. My parents think hez so much better than Pastor Dave, who used 2 make evry1 fall asleep /w his sermons. Sumtimes I even think abut things he sed in church when im abut to do sumthing mean 2 my brother nd it stops me (for a minute neway) ☺

Posted 11/30 @ 10:33 PM by zbest

Tuesday, December 1

Tonight I was setting the table for supper when the phone rang. It turned out to be Cara's swim coach. Although Mom drifted off into the living room to talk to him, I could hear her side of the conversation.

"Cara's just taking advice she says you gave her," she said in the perky voice she uses with clients all the time. "Why? Do you think there's something wrong?"

After a few minutes, Mom said, "I don't think so. You don't know my daughter as well as I do, Coach. She's just going through a rough patch."

When she came back into the kitchen to hang up the phone, her face had changed totally, and she didn't even look at me. Instead, she grabbed her cell phone and headed for her bedroom, which meant she was probably going to call Dad.

"Megan, have you noticed anything unusual about your sister?" she asked as soon as she came back out. But Cara came in the front door at that very second, so thankfully I didn't have to tell. Our kitchen has become like a war zone lately.

After supper (meatloaf and mashed potatoes for me, Mom, and Dad; only green beans for Cara), I was *dismissed* to my room. Of course, I snuck back out on the steps to hear what they were talking about.

"Cara, Coach Knepper called me. He thinks you have an eating disorder," Mom said.

"What? He's crazy. Everyone knows he gets all bent out of shape when we lose a meet." Cara was indignant, a pretty good performance considering he clearly had grounds for thinking that. I checked her stash of junk food the other day, and it's still there, so add that to the list of bizarre behavior. I mean, who would keep that stuff under their bed when they're refusing to eat regular food?

"I'm taking you to the doctor as soon as possible," Mom said. "There's something going on when a girl won't eat anything besides vegetables." (And, I wanted to add, as many cupcakes and candy bars as she can buy without you knowing it.)

"I'm fine! Daddy, are you going along with this?" (You know Cara's upset when she calls him *Daddy* instead of Dad.)

Dad's voice is low and rumbly, so I couldn't really hear what he said, but I knew he was trying to be reassuring. I ducked back into my room just as Cara came stomping up the stairway.

Because our rooms are right next door to each other, I couldn't help hearing her closet door open—it has a squeaky hinge Dad can never get fixed, like the floorboard next to my bed that makes a noise every time I step on it. Cara was quiet for a long time, but then I heard her go back downstairs and out to the garage.

I'm <u>not</u> a snoop—really. Until recently, when I started thinking something was wrong with her, I only went in her room for real reasons, like trying to find something of mine, and I never would have gone out into the garage to see what she did. Her life is so in my face, I don't need to look for more reasons to think about her.

But tonight I did. I tiptoed down to the garage and saw the lid on one garbage can halfway off. When I opened it there was a bag inside, stuffed full of empty wrappers from all the candy and snacks Cara had stashed away in her room.
Posted 12/1 @ 10:12 PM

Congrats 2 Chats 3

Mebbe itz just a craze, like those different diets that come nd go, xpecially athletes will try nething. My former VBF at school wud only eat protein when she was playing soccer, but it dint help her game at all neway, nd now she's dropped off the team.
Posted 12/1 @ 10:30 PM by tennytrish

<mental hugs> Guyz r so difrent abut stuff like that, u kno? Zeb stuffs himself all the time nd neva worries abut getting fat, altho mebbe he shud 🙂 i wish I culd lose abut ten lbs. but I love to eat nd we have a housekeeper who makes supper 2 (otherwise it wud be takeout every nite), nd I always have seconds even tho my older sister sez I eat like a pig.
Posted 12/1 @ 11:02 PM by zo4u

We had a lecture 2day on eating disorders nd the nurse sed grlz use food 2 try 2 take control of sum part of their life
Posted 12/1 @ 11:31 PM by zbest

Wednesday, December 2

Our house has this way of groaning and whispering when no one's awake that used to make me so scared I would run over to Cara's room as fast as I could and crawl into bed with her no matter what time it was. At 3 o'clock this morning, when I was flipping from one side of my bed to the other thinking about everything that's been going on, I almost considered doing it again. But I didn't.

Mom *forgot* about taking Cara to the doctor, or at least she didn't call one. If she thought Cara would actually start eating normally after their talk and life would go back to the way it was, she got a wake-up call today.

We all went to the semifinal swim meet (think eight long, boring hours on bleachers surrounded by other parents gossiping about Coach Knepper, except for Dad who tries to change the subject whenever people get critical).

"Where's Calla?" Mom asked me. (See how they think my life should revolve around her like theirs does?)

I looked up from my paperback (you definitely need a supply of those at swim meets) and toward the pool. It was like being in the audience trying to find a single singer in a choir on a stage far away. Finally I saw some of her friends and, when she took off her swim cap, I pointed.

"Right there, next to the high dive," I told Mom.

She sucked in her breath. "Look how thin she is!"

She nudged Dad and whispered something in his ear, so he looked, too. His eyes got all squinty the way they do when he's trying to answer a really hard question, like "Why do people suffer?" After a few seconds, he swallowed and pressed his lips together in a line.

Lots of T2P2's friends gave her grief because she can eat anything and stay thin, but even I had to admit that the girl by the pool was less than thin—she was <u>wasted</u>. When it was her turn to swim, it was pathetic. All you could see were these skinny arms churning away behind everyone else.

Cara has always been the best at swimming—first place in every event, as you can imagine—but not today. Looking at her non-existent muscles, I would say that wasn't going to happen any time in the near future, either.

Cara's friends (i.e. every girl on the team) clustered around her after she got out of the pool, and I could tell they were trying to pretend it wasn't a big deal that she came in last. Watching them, I remembered when Mom took us shopping last weekend. Cara had thrown a fit because she couldn't have the way-too-expensive jeans she wanted.

"I have to have them! Everyone else is wearing them, and you promised if I got good grades, you'd get me some. Anyway, there's only one pair left in my size," she told Mom in her best persuasive voice. (I've learned much from that voice.)

I looked at the rack and saw the "Size o" above the space where the jeans had been hanging. I've always thought it was sort of bizarre to have a size that can't legitimately exist, but seeing Cara in her swimsuit today made me realize it <u>was</u> possible to be close to nothing.

So, of course, the whole way home from the swim meet was nothing but drama, with Dad all thoughtful and serious and Mom crying and telling Cara this was it, she was definitely going to the doctor, and Cara being both pathetically upset and incredibly nasty.

"There's nothing wrong with me, Mom," she sort of snapped/sniffed. "I'm on this diet the Olympic swimmers follow."

None of us pointed out to her that her swim times were getting worse because of this wonderful diet, or that she looked terrible. I put my earphones on and buried my nose in a book in an attempt to tune them out for the rest of the trip, but even that wasn't enough. Mom and Cara kept going back and forth, with Dad getting pulled in from time to time. Finally, Mom slumped down in her seat, and Cara pretended to look out her window. Both of them were crying.

We were supposed to put up our Christmas tree tonight when we got back, but everyone forgot about that. Selfish me—but I was so disappointed.
Posted 12/2 @ 9:44 PM

Congrats 2 Chats 2

<delicate cough> ahem, duz ur mom even kno wut an eating disorder is? When my former VBF went on the protein kick it turned out she got all kinds of vitamin deficiencies nd had 2 be on this special supplement for a month that made her really constipated (shared in strictest confidence). There was a movie on Lifetime abut this mom who was so clueless abut the eating disorder nd her daughter died. . . . maybe thaz not the best thing 2 tell u but someone needs 2 do sumthing 4 her!

How's Jeremy? Is Mark completely out of the picture?

Me loves my Zebby!
Posted 12/2 @ 9:55 PM by zo4u

I dunt think itz selfish—u r part of the family, 2!! Mebbe u shud have a serious talk with your mom abut wut u kno. Cara looked terrible in church last week. I don't get it tho, why is she keeping all that stuff in her closet? Mebbe she can't rilly completely starve herself nd needz 2 have sum calories?
Posted 12/2 @ 10:15 PM by zbest

Thursday, December 3

I tried *nicely* asking Cara if there was anything wrong today, but she acted like I was suggesting she'd been a homecoming queen reject. Jess told me her brother heard that Cara and Trip broke up, and it's true he hasn't been calling lately, but Cara doesn't seem to care.

That's not the only thing she doesn't care about. It used to be that most nights after supper she and I would veg out on the sofa, gathering strength to do our homework. We took turns choosing what to watch and each had our own end of the sofa, where we would keep our special pillow to lean on and magazines to flip through while we watched. Forget that now. All Cara wants to do is stretch out on the sofa, staring at the food channels and flipping through recipe books. (Is she more weird than normal at this point?)

Zoey, don't count on Jeremy as a possible BBF. Maritza and I discussed the guys in AAP, and her opinion is that if any of them have boyfriend potential, they hide it well. (Although secretly, of all the guys I know at school, he's my best bet.)

Maritza has become like Jess—when we're at AAP I'm a *good enough* friend since the other three girls are way out of her league (three seniors, two juniors, and one übergoth), but as soon as Jess is around, it's like the good old days when the two of them had conversations that didn't include me—while I was sitting right there!

Anyway, Jeremy is so caught up in his art (he can paint and draw), I think I could be amazingly beautiful and he wouldn't notice. The only interest he's shown in me is to look at the drawing of Zoey I was working on and say, "Hey, not bad. Is she a real person?" If you lived here, I might be worried, Zoey.

However, there is a new kid, Kyle, who just started coming to our youth group, and Lisa and I both think he is to die for: straight brown hair, brown eyes that are sort of crinkled up like he's laughing all the time, and a totally ripped body you can appreciate even in jeans and a sweater. Probably a stretch for me since already the other girls flock around him, but when we were making Christmas food baskets to hand out next week, he did seem like he deliberately brushed his hand against mine one time. Lisa's still on the rebound from her BBF, who broke up with her not too long ago after they'd been going out for a year, but she agrees he is too cute.

I think my parents are getting ready to do something about the no longer T2P2. Dad took Cara out for ice cream (I'm sure he was the only one eating) last night, and she came back all teary eyed. Of course nothing changed—she was back to salad only at school today.

So Mom, Dad, and I decorated the Christmas tree without her.
Posted 12/3 @ 8:31 PM

Congrats 2 Chats 3

Sumtimes, u have 2 take the initiative (SAT vocab word)! I say, go 4 it /w the nu guy, Kyle. <sounds of encouragement> my in-between sister culd win the weird category ne day, believe me. Think preppy goth if u will, nd u c the life I live. Every1 at our skool makez fun of me bcuz of her! (Did u know button-down shirts even came in black? She sewed a patch that sez "bite me" over the little alligator—I can't believe she dint get detention.) Of course, my rents think they r the biggest failures eva except most of their friends have kids equally bad. I'm like the only semi-normal one, but they sure can't pin their hopes on me!

I'm so lucky to have Zebby, my OTL (one true love, hez more than a BBF). 2day he downloaded all this poetry off the Internet nd read it to me during lunch when we were sitting under this tree by ourselves. I culdn't stop myself from giving him a big kiss! U need a boyfriend.
Posted 12/3 @ 9:15 PM by zo4u

Not so, Zo! grlz don't have 2 have a BBF 2 b happy—altho I admit my life is always better when I'm going out /w sum1 special. Lisa, I kno how u feel. My BBF of 2 years nd I broke up last year (Megan heard the whole sad story at camp) so now I'm a free spirit nd joyful instead of boyful. . . .
Posted 12/3 @ 10:09 PM by tennytrish

Eggy, Kyle is perfect 4 u. u shud invite him 2 the youth group Christmas party—don't b shy! U guyz wudnt believe how sweet he is!
Posted 12/3 @ 11:17 PM by zbest

Friday, December 4

Okay, so today might qualify as the most traumatic day of my life. It all started at lunch, when I noticed Cara wasn't there, and Jess told me her brother saw my parents come and get her right after first period. (Thank you, text messaging, the secret communication system of every high school, which teachers believe doesn't go on constantly just because they tell us we can't.)

When I got home, Mrs. B was waiting at our house. As soon as I saw her, major alarm bells started ringing in my head.

"Your mom and dad asked if I would come over," she said, and I could tell this was the beginning of a rehearsed conversation, like the ones adults use to tell you things you really don't want to hear.

"Where are they? Where's Cara?" I asked. My voice got all trembly, and I know my face was completely red. Luckily, I didn't cry in front of her.

"Everyone is fine. Your mom is going to call in a little bit. How about a snack? I trust your parents do believe in snacks after school?" she said, opening the fridge and starting to poke around inside.

I ran upstairs, where Casper was hiding under my bed like he does when he gets upset—I hope Mrs. B hadn't been mean to him before I got there. I pulled him out and pretended he was my lovey from when I was two years old and needed those kinds of things. Then the tears came because I had no idea what was going on, which is typical. Am I even part of this family? They treat me like such a baby!

brb—Mom's on the phone.

Wow. Cara is in the hospital, like admitted as a patient and everything—not just in the ER like I was when I broke my arm. I guess Mom and Dad came to school and told her there was no option, she was going to the doctor, and when they got there, the doctor decided she needed to stay in the hospital "for a few days."

Mom was way evasive when I asked her how sick Cara was and wouldn't tell me exactly why they admitted her—why can't I know what they know?

We only talked for five minutes because Mom was standing outside the hospital to use her cell phone, but she promised she and Dad would be home as soon as visiting hours end at eight. Hello! Why can't I visit, too? More later. . . .

Okay, so now it's nine and neither of them is home. I refuse to go downstairs with Mrs. B, who finally brought a tray upstairs and left it outside my door, announcing that she is a very good cook and I will be sorry if I miss the opportunity to taste for myself.

Finally, out of pure starvation, I did eat it (excellent spaghetti; I guess she makes her own noodles, too—it figures), but if Mom or Dad or Mrs. B think I'm going to spend one minute talking to her or pretending it's okay to have a babysitter when you're grown up and actually formerly called upon to babysit yourself, they're so WRONG! When I brought my plate back down and went to get a glass of milk, she was actually asleep on the sofa in the living room, with the TV blaring some Christmas special.

I couldn't help staring at our beautiful tree, which is "gold themed" this year, as per Mom's directive, and think about last year at this time, when I was so hoping for a dog as my Christmas present. At least that wish came true. But what is there to wish for now that has any chance of really happening?
Posted 12/4 @ 9:09 PM

Congrats 2 Chats 2

Thaz such a typical thing 4 rents, as if sum kind of *movie moment* iz going 2 make nething better <eye roll nd sounds of dramatic sigh> Did u ever c that movie *Someone Cares*? itz abut this lame famly where the grl gets befriended by this old grandmotherly type who then makes evrythin okay in her life. I bet u dint c it b/c it flopped nd u can guess y. I told my rents it wuz a stupid idea when my dad got asked 2 work on it, but just like u, no 1 thinks I have nething important 2 say.
Posted 12/4 @ 9:29 PM by zo4u

Im so sorry 4 u, Megan! I cant imagine wut I wud do if my brothr got put in the hospital, even if he is a pitb. I guess ur dad is saying a lot of prayers, rite? I hope u r okay nd mebbe u shud give Mrs. B a chance—if she's from France she mite have sum interesting experiences that culd at least cheer u up. Sumtimes after church she nd my mom talk nd seem to laugh a lot.
Posted 12/4 @ 10:00 PM by zbest

Monday, December 7

It's official: I have a Mrs. B overdose. I've seen her more than Mom or Dad these last few days, and even though I have to admit she has good intentions (and is a great cook), she's really starting to irritate me.

"Megan, I thought we could look at those slides together!" she said last night, plopping this old-fashioned projector down on the coffee table. Hello! She needs an immediate crash course on PowerPoint.

Before I could say no, she had everything set up, so I looked at about 100 slides of every picture she's ever painted, starting from her teenage years on. In other circumstances, it might have been okay because she is/was an amazing artist, but I was desperate for Mom to call the entire time so I could find out what's going on with Cara. They won't let me see her, which makes me think she's really sick.

Everyone in school was talking about it today. Jess keeps acting like an authority on psychiatry and giving me all kinds of advice, while Maritza is my *protector* and tells the annoying kids who try to ask me questions to go away. My sanctuary is the library, where Miss Alexander, the librarian, doesn't make me talk if I don't want to. She did pull out a book written by a girl with an eating disorder, which I started to page through, but then I couldn't stand it.

"This is just too much information," I told Miss Alexander, shutting it and sliding it back across her desk. She gave me a smile back that was part sympathy and part encouragement.

"I know, Megan. My sister has an eating disorder, a really bad one. You wouldn't think it would bother me so much because we don't even live together and she's a lot older than me, but it does," she said. I couldn't believe it.

Then when Dad got home, he came up and sat on my bed like he does when he knows I'm worried about something, or when he's worried about something and wants to let me know it.

"Eggy, I know what's going on with Cara must be hard on you, too," he said in his best pastor voice.

"I'm fine," I said, pretending Casper was way more interesting than him. (Mom and Dad are either so clueless or so upset, they've been letting Casper sleep on my bed at night—absolutely forbidden before, but we both love it!)

"Eating disorders are hard to understand," he said next.

Finally, someone tells me something!

"What kind of eating disorder does she have?" I asked. (I probably know more than him already thanks to our health teacher, who did this totally disgusting class on throwing up or starving yourself to the point of your hair falling out. Her *message* was that there are lots of different ways you can get an eating disorder.)

Dad looked surprised by my question. "The doctors said it was anorexia," he told me.

There was a big silence, and then, I admit it, the trembly feeling came in my throat and I had to ask him the question I'd been thinking about every single hour of the day:

"Is she going to die?"

"Oh no, Eggy, that's why she's in the hospital!" He kind of lunged at me and hugged me tight against him, and for a minute it was like the old days when he could always make me feel better about anything, just by holding me on his lap. (And yes, like the old days, I did cry really hard because now it wasn't something lame like a skinned knee or a bee sting that was bothering me. After all, if Miss Alexander, a grown-up, was bothered enough by a sick sister to tell a kid about it, how am I supposed to react?)

We sat there for a while and he let me sob and gave me lots of tissues while Casper tried to nose his way between us. Dogs have a special way of knowing when anyone's upset, and Casper's got more intuition than most in that department. Eventually, Dad told me I could see Cara on Thursday night, and that the doctors said she would probably only be there for another week.

"They want to do a family therapy session—you'll be part of that." I pulled away from him when he said that. "Our family is perfect!

Cara's the one who has a problem," I said. It's just like Cara to now be the best person at having problems, so we all have to focus on her. "Why do we need therapy?"

He sort of smiled, which made me think he hears that a lot in his work. "This is more to help us understand each other a little better, Eggy. Now, how about you and I say a prayer for Cara before you turn out the lights?"

If you've ever prayed about anything, or if you go someplace where they think you should pray, you know prayer is not something you can do on demand. It's the worse side of having a dad who's a pastor—worse than sitting through service almost every Sunday morning because you want to please him and worse than having everyone in the congregation watch everything you do and wear (even though your mom doesn't care about most things like that).

When I was little, we used to kneel by my bed and say prayers every night, which was nice, sort of a routine, but the idea of prayer-on-demand bothers me. Of course, as I was thinking this, I got bothered by feeling bothered, because I'm sure God doesn't appreciate these kinds of feelings.

Anyway, Dad called Mom up, and we both had to listen to him pray for about twenty minutes (honest, I kept sneaking looks at the clock on my computer, which was right behind him). Luckily, he didn't expect me to say anything, and Mom just cried, so once he stopped talking, we were done.

Am I a terrible person, or what?
Posted 12/7 @ 8:45 PM

Congrats 2 Chats 1

u r not terrible at all. Religion is sumthing personal, my dad sez, which is why he gets upset when people try nd make movies or TV shows abut their beliefs just so other people will want to join up. I notice u haven't mentioned ne boyz in a long time, has ur life gone tolly downhill? 2day my BBF told me he has sumthing special planned 4 X-mas—can't wait! <sounds of pretend panting> seriously, he is the most 1derful guy a grl culd want. He drivz me 2 skool evry day nd is way safe, plus he carries my backpack 4 me—iz that roMANtik or wut? (nd yes, Trish, I read ur post nd no, I'm not boy crazy, I mostly haven't had a decent guy in my life until now. . . .)
Posted 12/7 @ 9:02 PM by zo4u

Wednesday, December 9

Zoey, you are so lucky! If I had a BBF, maybe my life would be easier, although having a BBF didn't help Cara much. Trip doesn't seem to miss her one bit—I really could not believe this, but in the hall today I saw him with his arm around Tonya (traitor!!!).

Kyle hasn't shown any interest in me, even though I sit next to him whenever I can (in a casual sort of *Oh my gosh, there's an empty seat right next to you!* way). Last week at youth group, I wore lipstick and *borrowed* one of Cara's cute tops that is too big for her anyway now that she's lost so much weight. Lisa didn't think so, but I thought Kyle kept looking at her all evening. There's tree-trimming tomorrow night, so maybe something will happen there. . . .

Jeremy has actually been helping me a lot with my art in AAP, which just makes me realize how much better than me he is. Of course, his parents gave him art lessons as soon as he could pick up a crayon, though Mr. Walker says we have to think in terms of talent, not training. But I do think I'm getting better, and Mrs. B agrees, for what that's worth.

Now during AAP, Maritza mostly hangs out with the one guy and girl who are also photographers, but we've been sitting together at the beginning and end of each session, when Mr. Walker gives us *feedback* (i.e. a long boring speech about how important it is to concentrate and do our best). Maritza found out they give a teacher award through AAP, too, so I'm sure he's hoping for enough of us to win so he can get it.

On the days when I don't have AAP, Mrs. B agreed to come over and cook supper for me while Mom and Dad are at the hospital. To be honest, those days are almost more peaceful since Mrs. B and I talk about art and food and all the different places she's lived—no mention of Cara. (I still haven't visited Cara— apparently the doctors decided she *wasn't ready* to have visitors besides Mom and Dad. Ahem . . . I'm her sister, not some random *visitor*!)

At school I am now a target for every stupid question and comment about eating disorders ever invented. Even Cara's friends seem to have turned against her.

"So does your sister eat <u>anything</u>?" Tonya asked me today. "Or does she stuff herself and then barf everything up like that movie on TV?" She had this big smirk on her face and her hands on her hips, blocking my way in the hall.

Tonya is about six feet tall and one of those sarcastic girls who can make you feel like you want to melt into the floor. To add to my humiliation/guilt/fear, Maritza was by my side since we were walking to AAP. But she surprised me by linking her arm through mine and giving Tonya this classic Maritza sideways look.

"What's the matter, Tonya? Worried Cara's going to come back and snatch Trip away?" she asked.

It's true that Tonya has been hanging out with Trip all the time, but I couldn't believe Maritza was brave enough to say something like that. Anyway, enough about school.

Mrs. B's personality has really changed—maybe she feels she has some kind of purpose in life now other than spying on her neighbors. I even found out she has one small glass of wine at dinner every night. Of course, Mom and Dad strictly prohibit me from trying alcohol, even though Mrs. B says it's common practice for even little kids to drink it in France. Every now and then she lets me have a little sip because she thinks it's important to know what different wines taste like—but I'm sworn not to tell Mom or Dad. Who would have thought Mrs. B could be so cool?

Tomorrow, instead of coming home after school, Mom is picking me up for the aforementioned (back at you, vocabulary word) family therapy session. Sounds like a really bad idea some grown-up thought of because he didn't know how else to make girls with eating disorders better.
Posted 12/9 @ 7:19 PM

Congrats 6 Chats 3

Hey, out here evry1 is in therapy, even me. I have my own

therapist who sumtimz duz rilly cool stuff like yoga nd listening 2 music. <sounds of peaceful chanting> Thaz why I want 2 b a therapist sum day—evry1 telz me Im already a gr8 listener.

Pretty soon I will see wut my sweetie got me 4 Xmas. it duz put sum pressure on me, tho. Wut do u get 4 a guy who mite b investing major bucks in a gift 4 u?
Posted 12/9 @ 7:45 PM by zo4u

The best present I got my ex-BBF wuz a puppy. His mom sed it wuz okay ahead of time, so I went 2 the Animal Rescue place nd picked 1 out. U kno guyz r so unsentimental, but he wuz rilly happy, nd of course now he has a reminder of me evry day . . . even tho we broke up.
Posted 12/9 @ 8:00 PM by tennytrish

Do u rilly think Kyle mite like me?
Posted 12/9 @ 8:21 PM by zbest

Thursday, December 10

So I just got home from the hospital and will probably write about ten pages, because I'm so upset and there's nobody—and I mean nobody—who could possibly understand how I feel right now. (That's why I appreciate you guys.) Today is now the new official "Worst Day of My Life," and who knows what else might happen before I turn out the lights, snuggle next to Casper, and sleep straight through until morning.

Before we went in the hospital, Mom told me there was something I needed to know, and that *something* was that Cara has a tube in her nose so food can go through it right into her stomach.

"You mean like in the movies when someone can't eat?" I asked.

Mom kind of crumpled up her face, and I knew she was trying to think of a way to answer me without telling the complete truth but not outright lying.

"Yes, it's that kind of tube, but it's just to supplement what Cara's eating so she'll get better faster," she finally said. "We thought it might upset you to see her like that, so we waited until now to bring you in. Look, I got a present for you to give her!"

She leaned over and fished something out of the backseat. It was all packaged in a shiny bag, sort of like her gift baskets. You won't believe it, but it was the body lotion and bath gel set I specifically requested for Christmas last year and didn't get!

Okay, I got Casper, which is way better, but when Mom saw the bath lotion and gel on my list back in December, she'd wrinkled her nose and said, "Eggy, that store is so overpriced! You can go to the drugstore and get the same thing for a third of the cost."

So this afternoon I just sat there, holding the basket and wondering if she had even the faintest memory of making me feel so shallow and materialistic.

Finally, she saw the look on my face. "You know Cara really wanted that for Christmas, so I thought it would be a nice pick-me-up," she said, sort of lame.

"Mom, *I* was the one who wanted it for Christmas!" I wanted to scream, but of course Cara is sick enough to have a tube in her nose, so I didn't.

That was just the beginning of an awful evening. It really was worse than I imagined to see my sister with this tube dangling out of her nose and looking even thinner than before. She was like those Halloween skeletons, with a happy expression on her face but only bones for the rest of her body.

Then we all had to eat dinner together, which made me actually wish I was with Mrs. B instead, since at least I'd be eating good food. This was awful hospital food, and Cara pushed it away before she even took a bite. I wouldn't blame her for not eating any of it, but without her stash of candy and whatnot, that tube is her only source of nutrition.

There wasn't much to talk about, either. I tried to answer Cara's questions about school in a sort of funny way, and when she asked about Trip, of course I didn't mention he was hanging out with a new girl every day (including her former best friend).

When Mom and Dad talked to her, they kept calling her "Calla" and trying to pretend like they were all cozy and everything and that her obsession with food didn't bother them. (All Cara talked about was how many calories the hospital was forcing her to eat, how gross the food was, and how unfair the doctors were—suddenly I was glad they hadn't been bringing me along on visits.)

But then, after I thought we had gone through the worst part of the evening, we got ushered into this ugly little room with institutional furniture (uncomfortable but indestructible) and magazines about ten years old. We sat and waited forever until the doctor and another person came in.

"Hi! I'm Dr. M!" the doctor told me. "My last name is so hard to pronounce I just tell everyone to call me that. You must be Megan." He stuck out his hand, so I had to shake it, along with the other person's, who turned out to be a social worker. The doctor had a ponytail and a pierced ear, and the social worker would have been a goth at my school—she had black/purple hair and was dressed in all black, even her jewelry (bangle bracelets, clunky necklace, and dangly earrings).

We had to get in sort of a circle so we could see each other's faces, and then Dr. M started talking about "Cara this" and "Cara that" and how we all needed to really appreciate what she was going through and how hard things were for her. (Excuse me— she just got MY Christmas present!)

After he went on about that for ten minutes, he looked right at me and said, "So, Megan, I understand there's a lot of tension between you and your sister."

If someone knocked me right off the sofa, I wouldn't have been as upset as I was then, but before I could say a word, Mom jumped to her feet.

"Just a minute, Dr. M. There's not 'a lot of tension' between Megan and Cara—they're normal sisters. I see both of them provoke each other at times."

The doctor looked at her with this sort of smile and said, "Tell me what 'normal' means to you, Mrs. Leeman." I could almost hear the psychiatric wheels grinding away in his head.

It was all I could do not to cry. If Cara's eating disorder was my fault, that would make me a really bad person. To be honest, I never thought she and I fought that much because she was always the best at everything, including arguments. I learned early on it wasn't worth it to battle with her.

"So, when Cara comes home, do you think the two of you can get along better?" Dr. M asked when we were all done and getting ready to leave. This time, Dad frowned and crossed his arms over his chest.

"You know, Dr. M," he said in a voice I've only heard him use when he gets really frustrated with the board at church. "I really don't like the sound of that."

Dr. M's eyebrows just lifted a little, and he shrugged. "Clearly, there are issues that need to be talked about in your family, Mr. Leeman."

"That might be true, but one of those issues is not whether Megan will try and 'get along' with her sister, as you suggested. She makes plenty of effort as it is."

That was all it took for Cara to push past everyone and yank open the door. "See, I told you how things are!" she said. "Everyone makes excuses for her!"

Before anyone could stop her, she pulled out of Mom's attempt at a hug and stomped off, slamming the door behind her. The air in the room felt too hot to breathe, and for a second, everyone seemed frozen in place. Then Dad opened the door and went after Cara, while Mom collapsed against the social worker, sobbing. Dr. M shook his head and went through the doorway with Cara's chart in one hand, fingering his earring with the other.

As you can imagine, it was a bad ride down on the elevator. Mom was mad at Dad for provoking Cara, and he was mad at Dr. M for creating problems where there weren't any. Secretly, I was on Dad's side, since I had already decided I was never going back to a family therapy session again. If anything, Dr. M had <u>created</u> problems for us in the one hour we spent with him!
Posted 12/10 @ 11:30 PM

Congrats 2 Chats 1

Hey grl, dunt let it get 2 u. my mom had 2 come 2 therapy /w me one day, so I just made up a bunch of stupid stuff like she won't let me stay out late on weekends nd she likes my sister better so we'd have sumthing 2 talk about. (My real problem is the kids at my school, who are tolly ignorant nd just mean, but nobode can do nething abut that.) After we left therapy my mom was crying nd everything, nd I told her none of it wuz true cause I nu if I didn't say sumthing the therapist wud try nd do just what that guy did. So then she rilly did get mad at me nd sed she wuz going 2 switch my therapist, which is wat she did. Now evrythin is fun nd cool. Mebbe ur sis can get a btr doctr <expression of thoughtful reflection>
Posted 12/10 @ 11:55 PM by zo4u

CHAPTER 10

Friday, December 11

Last night I couldn't sleep because I was so upset about what happened with that stupid psychiatrist—or maybe he's not so stupid after all and this really is my fault. Wouldn't that be too weird, with me thinking how superior Cara was in just about everything?

My feelings must have been on my face at school, or at least during AAP while we were waiting for Mr. Walker to arrive. Maritza had to miss because of a doctor's appointment, so I was listening to music and kind of zoned out when this paper airplane sailed over to me. I opened it up, and there was a picture of Casper, which was too cute. (Last week, I had showed Jeremy my screensaver picture, and he agreed Casper could be a model kind of dog.) Underneath, he wrote, "Doggone it, you need to smile!"

As soon as I saw it, I completely skipped my trembly voice precry and ran out in the hallway, sobbing. Jeremy came running after me.

"Hey, that was supposed to be a joke," he said, giving me a tissue.

For the first time I noticed his smell, kind of a cold-air smell, like in winter right before it's going to snow. It's one of my favorite smells (next to cherry vanilla) because I love snow.

"It's okay," I said. (Could I possibly have sounded more lame?) "Things are just a little . . ."

I couldn't even think of how to describe what I was going through without sounding completely insane. No one else in our whole school has a sister in the hospital with a tube in her nose that could possibly be their fault.

"Rough?" he asked, but he said it sort of like a dog barking, which sounds corny, but suddenly I was looking at the picture (which I was still holding) and smiling, then laughing.

"That's a really bad joke," I said, "but thanks for the picture and for making me laugh. I guess you heard about my sister being in the hospital and all—that seems to be the big buzz around school these days."

He shrugged. "It'll be old news in a week. You know how that goes."

"I guess," I said. I didn't want to stare at him, but I couldn't help it. He looked so different than all the times we've been together before—taller and cuter and cuddly, kind of like the flannel shirt he was wearing. That was when Mr. Walker decided to come down the hall, so I sort of nodded at Jeremy, and we went back inside. I ducked into my seat, reminding myself to call Jess as soon as I got home and ask her to find out everything her brothers know about him.

A few hours later, after chicken cordon bleu with Mrs. B (and the smallest sip of the wine she had brought over, which tasted fresh and cold), Jess called back.

Here's what she said: "Okay, so I got everything I could from my brothers, but you totally owe me, Eggy, because now they think *I* like him!" Jess sounded more excited than she usually does when she talks to me, so I could tell she thought Jeremy had boyfriend potential. "None of them are friends with Jeremy since he's sort of mysterious, and I had to ask all kinds of questions before I found anything useful, but you know Charlie caves under pressure. Anyway, he told me Jeremy lives with his dad since his parents are divorced, and his dad is some kind of famous author, you can probably look him up on the Internet. And he is so not gay because he's dating a girl in college, but maybe you can steal him away! Me and Maritza need to do a total makeover on you, girl—pronto!"

Of course, what she said fits perfectly with my life right now—you put something on your wish list, and it instantly turns out not to be even a remote possibility.

Some other not-likely-to-happens:
• Cara would wake up tomorrow completely better
• I would create something amazing and win the art contest
• Jess and/or Maritza would decide to be my VBF
• And, of course, Jeremy would become a true OTL candidate

But it turns out he's just being a nice person who's trying to cheer me up, something I sort of suspected already. I mean, he always gets this dreamy look in his eyes and a slow smile when he talks about drawing so that tells you what he feels dreamy about. Unlike Maritza, who doesn't hesitate to tell me she wants to win the final AAP art contest so everyone will see how good she is, Jeremy really wants me to be as good as him in art. I guess that adds up to "too good to be true."

Sigh.

We did go to this exhibit at the community college gallery last weekend with AAP, which was kind of interesting—this woman uses pastels and then varnishes over the top of it, then adds more color and varnish. It was too cool! We even got to talk to the artist, who is someone I could totally imagine being; she teaches art classes and has her own studio and a really unique

style in the way she dresses. I'm betting she didn't grow up with a T2P2.
Posted 12/11 @ 9:23 PM

Congrats 6 Chats 4

Well, now that u r talking abut Jeremy, I will say that Kyle is rilly nice like that, 2. Do u still like him, becuz if u rilly don't mebbe I will go out /w him just 2 the movies.
Posted 12/11 @ 10:00 PM by zbest

Heydah! Wow, having sum1 be that nice 2 u is a real plus, nd altho I dint post b4 I think itz terrible wut that psycho doctor sed 2 u. my VBF went 2 a therapist who tole her she needed 2 stop lying 2 evry1 nd being so selfish. U can imagine how her parents reacted becuz she rilly wuz depressed nd needed help.
Posted 12/11 @ 10:32 PM by tennytrish

Hey grl don't give up so eze! <mental hug> duz ur dad ever talk abut miracles bcuz they do happen. My mom's friend had cancer nd got completely healed after she started meditating. Mebbe u shud try that? Everyone said my OTL had a BGF b4 we started going out, but we were meant 2 b bcuz he dropped her 4 me.
Posted 12/11 @ 10:45 PM by zo4u

Even if I don't have a BF, it doesn't matter when I have good friends like you guys! Lisa, I gave up on Kyle when he picked you to be his partner at the tree-trimming party. It was clear he has the hots for you. Go for it!!!

I wish we all lived near each other and could do things together,

and that you three could meet each other finally. You would see what I already know—you rock!
Posted 12/11 @ 11:12 PM by sistrsic92

Saturday, December 12

So bummed . . . I got the total yucks that everyone's been passing around. I have a fever and can't even think about eating because my stomach turns upside down whenever I move. So here I am propped up on the sofa with Casper, an untouched glass of ginger ale, and Mom's laptop, trying to find something to watch on TV. Obviously, I won't be able to make it to the youth group Christmas party. Does my life suck or what?
Posted 12/12 @ 8:17 PM

Congrats 2 Chats 0

Monday, December 14

Jess won't let up on me about the makeover, which would have taken place this weekend if I wasn't still feeling so sick, so I decided to let her try it. I called Mom at lunch, and she called Mrs. B, and it was decided I could go to Jess's house after school. Of course, Maritza came along, too.

Since my parents spend every evening at the hospital (which is not that far from our house), I'm sure Casper is the only person who cares that I'm not around. (Good news, though, I think: Cara is coming home in four days!)

Anyway, Jess's mom picked us up and asked me all kinds of

embarrassing questions about Cara until Jess told her to stop. Mrs. B said she would come and get me at 8 PM, which was a little scary because her driving in the daytime is what she calls "European style." I'm not sure she sees all that well—driving in the dark with her will be even more of an adventure.

So Jess and Maritza had four hours to create a whole new me. They started with makeup. Jess has a whole drawerful, so she had to get all the right colors figured out and organize the brushes. Meanwhile, Maritza combed out my hair and straightened it and then looked through the closet for something *sexy* I could borrow. (Jess and I have always been about the same size on top, so add that to my previous SF vs. BF debate, even though her style is the opposite of mine.)

I have to say it was incredible to see myself with shiny, smooth hair and really dark eyes and dangly earrings and lips all pink and wet. The point being, it wasn't really me in the mirror, no matter how much they assured me it was. It would take an hour to do all this stuff every morning, but I guess they do.

Mrs. B looked at me sideways when I got in the car and took a big drag of her cigarette (another downside of spending time with Mrs. B—she smokes about a pack of these disgusting European cigarettes a day).

"You look very attractive," she said. At least she seems to feel sorry for me since Cara's problems began. She isn't at all critical of anything Casper or I do, and sometimes her eyebrows go up ever so slightly when I tell her what's happening in my life.

Mom and Dad gave me one of those *isn't that nice, you had fun with your friends* smiles when they got home. Seeing the sadness quickly come back on their faces, I stopped focusing on my looks and asked about Cara, although inside I forgot about being relieved that she's coming home in time for Christmas and got really mad at her all over again. Why is she so determined to make them suffer?

It turns out I *must* go to family therapy again, because we all have to help her when she comes home. As if our lives don't already revolve around her!

I went upstairs and threw the makeup Jess gave me in the trash can, then fished it back out because she'll be majorly upset if I don't at least try it. Casper is the only being who truly understands how I feel right now (and my blog buds, of course, and maybe Mrs. B). I'm sorry—I don't think a nice God would let such bad things happen to our family, no matter what Dad says.

Dad thinks I don't know, but I heard people whispering about Cara after church last week, wondering why a PK would ever have such problems. I don't know how Dad does it—he is still nice to everyone, but he's not as happy as he used to be, obviously, and sometimes he comes home from meetings with the church council and goes right into his study without saying a word to any of us.

Mom is luckier—she can kind of take off work when she needs to, especially around this time of year, when buying a house is the last thing most people are thinking about. That doesn't mean she sits around all day waiting for visiting hours, but she does spend a lot of time talking to Cara's therapists and reading about eating disorders online.

I heard the two of them murmuring in Dad's study last night and found out that someone had suggested the church get an interim pastor while Dad is going through all this.

"Maybe it's not such a bad idea, hon. You can't keep pushing yourself like this, making visits and teaching class and writing sermons and then being there as much as Cara needs you," Mom said. "I'm worried about you, too."

"What kind of example would I set if I just gave up on helping others because our family has hit tough times?" he said.

Hey, God, if You haven't noticed, Dad could really use a little support right now!
Posted 12/14 @ 10:30 PM

Congrats 2 Chats 1

Hi formerly sick 1! We all missed u at the Xmas party. I did hang out a lot /w Kyle nd u r right, he is so sweet, but of course if I dint have ur blessing ahead of time I wud have tolly ignored him. Neway, he nd I agree ppl at church r just ignorant when they say things abut ur sistr. Kyle has a cousin who had a rilly bad eating disorder nd he sez his whole family was so worried. Mebbe u shud talk 2 him?
Posted 12/14 @ 10:46 PM by zbest

CHAPTER 11

Thursday, December 17

Lisa, I'm so happy for you—Zoey and Trish, if you could see her with Kyle, you would think they are one of those perfect couples who look so happy and cute together. Speaking of cute, I saw Jeremy in the hallway today. . . .

We just said *hey* and kept going, but seeing him reminded me of the picture he drew, which then reminded me that he is already taken, so I got tears in my eyes and had to run to the bathroom. It was hard to blot them up without ruining my mascara, but I managed and told myself no matter what, I would not let myself get too upset. If I did, that would remind me of what happened at our family therapy session last night at the hospital, and then I might lose control completely. I needed my blog pals so badly!

So, it went like this: Dr. M was in charge again, but this time there was a dietician and a social worker there. Things started out

pretty boring until the dietician whipped out a paper with Cara's
meal plan. Then it got downright awful.

First, Cara's face looked like <u>Mt. Rushmore</u>, all stubborn and
hard. I instantly thought that offering to make <u>Christmas cookies</u>
with her when we got home wasn't such a great idea. Then, she
crossed her still-skinny arms over her chest.

"There is no way on God's green earth I'm eating 1,700 calories a
day," she said.

"Calla," my dad started in his gentle voice, but she turned on
him, looking like those lions you see on TV that sail through the
air to attack the innocent animal who will be their next meal.

"You're <u>not</u> my real dad," she said. "So you can't tell me what
to do."

That might have possibly been the most hurtful thing anyone
could ever say to him, worse than the people at church who
gossip and worse than the people who scream at him because
they're secretly mad at God. You would never know he wasn't
her *real dad* because he treats her exactly the same as he
does me.

My heart started pounding, and before I knew it I stood up and
squinted my eyes as mean as I could at her. "Well, if you're so
concerned with not eating too much, maybe you should get rid of
all those snacks you keep in your closet! But maybe I'm not your
<u>real</u> sister, either."

I was shaking after I said this, and the room seemed like it was shrinking, so I ran outside and down the hall, where I knew there was a bathroom. Now my mascara was dissolved all over my face. Mom found me and just sat on the floor next to me and hugged me.

"Why does she have to be so mean?" I asked. "It's not like she even remembers her *real* dad—you told me that."

"Eggy, these are tough times," Mom answered, kind of rocking me back and forth a little.

But I think we both suddenly realized that we were sitting on the floor of a hospital bathroom (hello) and got up at the same time. "That's gross," we said, almost in unison, then we both smiled— a little smile, but it made me feel better.

Still, I refused to go back and *talk things out* with the formerly T2P2.

We drove home in silence—or rather, we drove home without speaking. Dad, who has a marvelous voice, sang the liturgy from church over and over, which was more comforting than I ever would have thought possible.

Posted 12/17 @ 8:44 PM

Congrats 2 Chats 2

Wut a b——! (I kno ur dad is a minster so don't want 2 offend u, but rilly!) it must b the starvation is affecting her brain, b/c ur dad soundz like he is awesum, nd u 2. I hope those smart a** therapists realized they don't kno everything! I can so imagine my bro doing something similar. He wrekd the car last year nd

instead of being punished it wuz suddenly all abut the
emotional trauma he had gone through.

Hey, thnx 4 bing so nice abut me nd Kyle. I kno u decided 2 go 4
Jeremy, but lots of grlz at my skool get in major fites over guyz.
Posted 12/17 @ 9:00 PM by zbest

Believe it or not, Mom told me the doctor dint even talk to Cara
abut wut I sed bcuz *hoarding behavior* is very typical of girls /w
eating disorders.
Posted 12/17 @ 9:24 PM by sistrsic92

Saturday, December 19

So Cara has been home for a day now, and we still haven't talked.
I don't care, I'm going to avoid her all weekend and stay after
school every day next week if I can or even go over to Mrs. B's
house to get away from her. Speaking of whom, there'll be no
more really delicious meals every night, but she did call me over
after school yesterday and heated up this little sliver of quiche as
a snack. Mmm.

"I made one for your family, but I thought I'd make an extra for
myself and give you a piece to taste test," she said, sipping her
glass of wine. (She tells me she sips the same glass all evening.
At first I didn't believe her, but I have since learned it's true.)

I took teeny bites, dragging out the time with her as long as
possible (imagine that), and then wished I liked wine so I could
drink a whole glass of it before I went back to my house. Instead,
I eventually had to take the whole quiche, wrapped up in this
beautiful dishcloth, and carry it over to the war zone.

When Mom heated it up, the quiche was so good I couldn't believe Cara would turn it down, but that's exactly what she did. As you can imagine, this sparked a battle, only all the action was quiet: Mom sighing, me slamming my fork and plate in the sink once I was done, and Dad clearing his throat every ten seconds, a nervous habit he rarely shows.

If I thought it was hard to be the sister of a T2P2, I was wrong. It's so much worse to be the sister of someone who is slowly ruining the entire family. I hate her.
Posted 12/19 @ 6:10 PM

Congrats 2 Chats 1

Rite on. sistrs r 2 strange, u think they wud b ur best friend nd the 1 person who wud help u no matter wut, but my in-btween sis nd I are sumtimes worst enemies. Hatred is a kind way of putting it <sounds of violent emotion> I 1der if Jeremy will get u an Xmas present? 😊 Let me kno!
Posted 12/19 @ 7:36 PM by zo4u

Monday, December 21
I can't believe it's possible to have the Best Day of My Life 😊 (to date) in the middle of the worst time of my life 😞. Brace yourself!

Today was an AAP day, so of course I knew I would see Jeremy and wore the shirt Jess insisted I borrow this weekend (her *Improve Eggy* campaign is still in full force). Actually, this is my favorite piece of clothing she owns, so I didn't put up a fuss, although secretly I think it looks way better on her. It's this kind of delicate material with lace around the sleeves and it matches the *Pucker Pink* lipstick she gave me for my birthday last year perfectly. (Thinking back, I believe her campaign started a long time ago.)

Anyway, Jeremy didn't seem impressed by the shirt or the lipstick because he didn't look at me any longer or any different than he usually does. When Maritza came in and noticed this lack of interest, she gave him her evil eye. But then Mr. Walker asked to see her portfolio, so I kind of sat down a few seats in front of Jeremy, where the drawing/painting crowd hangs out.

Finally, at the end, when I was getting my stuff together, Jeremy took this sketch out of his portfolio and handed it to me. Maritza saw him standing next to me and gave me one of her *I told you so* looks.

I couldn't believe it—the sketch was a picture of me! It was so close to what I really look like it could be a photograph, only black-and-white. He got the exact way my hair flips up a little at the ends and the few freckles across my cheeks that stay with me year round and even the way my eyes sometimes look when I'm reading a book, even though I'm not (a look I've also seen on my face in spontaneous photographs).

"So what do you think?" he asked.

"I think you could be really successful at doing that sidewalk art in New York City, where they draw your picture on the spot. You made me look really good!"

As soon as I said it, I hoped it wasn't a terrible insult, since I know some people think those guys aren't *real* artists. I also thought many people, male and female alike, would respond with reassurance and a false comment like, "Oh, but you really do look as good as the picture!" but Jeremy did not. Instead, he took it back and studied it for a minute.

"You're right," he said. "You're smiling too much. You haven't looked this happy in a long time."

I got this feeling like I used to get when I was little and Dad took me to the playground and let me go on those push merry-go-rounds forever. Sometimes I would feel sick because I went around so much, but the sickness was nowhere near the excitement I felt over the world being a blur and the wind in my face and the feeling that I could take off and fly at any moment.

That's how Jeremy made me feel right then. And that's when I knew it: on some level, he is interested in me! True, artists are interested in other people all the time, or at least that's the secret Mrs. B told me one time when she and I were watching one of those really old black-and-white movies she likes on TV.

"You never know when a smile on a little girl's face or a man's hat might be something you want to re-create," she said, so for the rest of the movie we played this game to see who could notice the most unusual thing.

To think—of all the people he could watch, Jeremy picked me. He noticed something not even my mom and dad did—I am not so happy these days. Then there was the time he had put into drawing the picture, which was more than anyone else was dedicating just to me, Mrs. B aside.

"I still want it!" I said, snatching it back and hoping I leaned close enough for him to smell Jess's "Positively Peach" body splash. (Never have I wanted to smell like a fruit, but she insisted studies have shown that boys like it.)

Now, you won't believe I ever had the confidence to do this, but once I had the picture back, I held out my hand like we do in church when we exchange the sign of peace.

"Thank you so much. I know you have a girlfriend, so don't take me the wrong way. We shake hands or hug in church every Sunday with people we care about."

"Umm . . . okay. So what are you, all religious or something?" he asked. "I mean, I know your dad is a priest—"

"Pastor," I corrected. "Priests don't get married."

"Oh."

I gently put the picture in my portfolio after looking at it again. I so wished he didn't have a girlfriend and would make me smile again.

And then, as if he were reading my mind, he said, "I don't have a girlfriend. Were you checking?"

I smiled and ducked my head, but a thought came into my mind.

I snuck a quick peak at his eyes. "You knew about my dad, so you must have checked up on me, too."

We both laughed, kind of uncomfortable, until Mr. Walker realized we were still there and came over to see what was going on.

"You guys are going to miss the late bus," he said, checking his watch. (Translation: "My teaching day is over, but I can't leave until you two do.")

"I drive myself," Jeremy said, and I told Mr. Walker that I had a ride, too, but we knew enough to pack up our stuff and head out. My heart was still jump-roping super-fast in my chest at the thought of Jeremy considering me kind of nice looking, and that dizzy merry-go-round feeling was like a buzz in my head.

The day got even better, though.

When I went home, I scooped the mail out of the mailbox like I always do and saw a red envelope with my name on it. I didn't recognize the handwriting, but something told me this was not an envelope I wanted anyone in my family to know about, so I dropped the rest of the mail on the stand in the hallway and dashed upstairs.

Of course, Cara would never notice anyway: she was busy fixing her own dinner, which was special and different from ours, while the food channel blared in the background. (Aside: we have started talking again, but she asked Mom and Dad to put a lock on her door! They told her no but made me promise I would respect her privacy and not go in without permission. As if I want to know any more than I already do about her eating habits.)

Casper ran up the stairs right behind me, and when he jumped up on my lap I could barely open the envelope. I saw the return address was New Hampshire and there is only one person I know from New Hampshire: Mark, adorable tennis player extra-ordinaire. So imagine my feelings as I tried to control a wriggly Westie with one hand and open the envelope with another.

Not only was there a funny Christmas card inside, but it had a tennis theme: "Hope Santa will make a racquet at your house this year!" There was a picture of Santa trying to stuff himself down a chimney with a sack full of tennis racquets.

Mark also wrote a note on the inside of the card saying he had lost my address and just tracked me down on the Internet through Dad. Better yet, he gave me his screen name!

Normally, I might *allow* Mom to pry the truth out of me and spill all about the card during supper, but, as usual, no one seemed to notice I was even there.

"Come on, Calla, have some pasta," Dad said, pushing the bowl toward her. On Cara's plate was a heap of mushrooms stir-fried in artificial butter—I will say no more.

She shoved the bowl back at him and just kept eating those mushrooms one by one until we all finished our meals and got up from the table.

Luckily, Mrs. B surprised me by showing up after supper with all the ingredients for Christmas cookies. Although I was suspicious that it was prearranged (Mom and Dad were going shopping and to a concert at another church), part of me felt sort of relieved. This is something Cara, Mom, and I normally do, but I could tell no one was even thinking about baking this year. It's bad enough that we're going to Washington for Christmas, but that doesn't mean we can't do some of the normal things.

As soon as Cara saw Mrs. B, she rolled her eyes, sighed as loudly as she could, and went upstairs. If Mrs. B was offended, she didn't show it. Taking a big sip from the glass of wine she had cupped in one hand, she started arranging the supplies on the counter.

"So, what exciting things happened to you today?" she asked.

At first I thought it was too pathetic to talk about boys with my really old neighbor, who has no idea of what teenage life is like, but then I realized that other than Jess (who would have to wait to see the evidence firsthand), Mrs. B was my best bet. I ran upstairs and got my portfolio and told her the whole story about Jeremy then laid the red envelope on the table. She read the card, her eyebrows raised. "*Deux amours*—not bad."

"They're not in love with me!" I told her, but she gently arranged the picture and the card on the table, studying both.

"I don't know, you have definitely made an impression on someone," she said, taking a sip from her glass.

I had to put my head down and pretend to be looking for the mixer to hide the smile on my face.

Posted 12/21 @ 8:23 PM

Congrats 2 Chats 4

Omg, omg, omg!! u r so lucky! Ur day was defin8ly btr than mine! Turns out my OTL (shud I make that *ex*?) thinks I have sum gr8 desire 2 see his favorite group the Headbangers, so he got us tickets for this weekend—thaz the present he's been making such a big deal about! After weeks of w8ting, I can't believe it wuz sumthing more 4 him than me!

Posted 12/21 @ 9:10 PM by zo4u

Jeremy sounz like such a gr8 guy—one of the girls in my cabin at tennis camp told me Mark is a player, altho mebbe she wuz just jealous. U kno how grlz can b abut that. I dint think ud hear from him again, which is why I didn't tell u.

Posted 12/21 @ 9:16 PM by tennytrish

I heard those rumors at tennis camp, too, but Mark told me his ex GF's friends were there and had it in for him. He doesn't seem like a player—but who knows? Anyway, I don't mean to pretend I'm some super-desirable person just because I got stuff from two boys.

Posted 12/21 @ 10:05 PM by sistrsic92

U r so lucky—2 guyz interested in u! Kyle iznt surprised they rilly like u cuz u r gr8 nd he sez he can see why we r frenz.
Posted 12/21 @ 11:30 PM by zbest

CHAPTER 12

Tuesday, December 22

Jess was so excited when I showed her the card and the picture that she started screaming in the cafeteria, which majorly embarrassed me, but I can tell that now that I have male interest in my life, I am definitely her favorite. This, of course, makes Maritza insanely jealous, so she started hanging all over the boys at the lunch table next to ours with the hope that they would notice her. The lunch table is not a bad choice actually, since most of the popular guys from our class sit there, but that's the point—they're from our class. If they were interested in Maritza, they probably would have acted like it by now. (Not to mention that the cheerleader table is also next to ours.)

"You have to get a picture of Mark," Jess told me. "That way we can help you choose which guy to go after."

"Why pick one?" Maritza shrugged, taking this slow, sexy bite out of her apple while staring at Ethan, this really cute guy who also happens to be class president.

Although I pretended to be listening to Jess debate Jeremy vs. Mark, I couldn't help watching Maritza. She has this way about her that makes everything she does seem special, even when she smiles. Sometimes at night I look in the bathroom mirror and try to copy her, but I don't have smoky eyes and long curly hair like her, so I look pretty pathetic.

Maritza is an incredible photographer, too. Looking at her pictures makes me want to tear up the lace collage I started last week—in fact, I did start to tear it up, and then I noticed that the rips looked sort of interesting, so I might try adding them to my future collages. Speaking of art, how will I survive without AAP (and Jeremy) until after Christmas break?
Posted 12/22 @ 5:56 PM

Congrats 2 Chats 3

Well, the concert wuz a bust nd Zeb dumped me 2 hang out mostly /w his friends. How can guys b so cruel? <sounds of distraught weeping>
Posted 12/22 @ 6:16 PM by zo4u

Oh sweetie, if he wuz ne kind of a real OTL he wud neva do sumthin like that 2 u. There r nicer guys around, I'm sure.
Posted 12/22 @ 7:03 PM by zbest

I agree—I'm sorry we culdn't talk longer but my mom makes me save my long-distance minutes thinking that at sum point she mite b far away nd I will have 2 call her. But Lisa is rite, u r so much

better than Zeb. If he chooses to treat u like that, itz his loss!
Posted 12/22 @ 8:30 PM by sistrsic92

Wednesday, December 23

Today is a sad(der) day because I have to say good-bye to Casper
(temporarily) tomorrow morning, since we'll be flying to
Washington. In anticipation, I've packed more books than clothes
in my suitcase. I hope I don't have to sit next to Cara on the
plane—imagine how she'll feel about the food or lack thereof.

When I asked Mom why he couldn't come along in one of those
cute doggie carriers, she reminded me that her dad (who totally
doesn't seem like my grandpa) doesn't like dogs, and that we
would be doing a lot of traveling once we got to Seattle. Of
course, Mrs. B now thinks Casper is the cutest thing around and
even bought this doggie Santa hat that is beyond adorable on
him! She volunteered to watch him while we're gone and whispered
in my ear that she would give him a lot of TLC. That made me
feel better, because I've concluded that Mrs. B must be lonely—
she doesn't have any kids, and all her relatives are dead. In fact,
Dad is spending Christmas Eve with her.

That makes me sad, too. (I mean, glad for Mrs. B but sad for
me.) Dad has to do church on both Christmas Eve and Christmas
morning, so he won't fly out until later in the day, but at least I
know Mrs. B has a special meal planned for him. Sad and
Christmas should not be used in the same paragraph.

Dad must have guessed I was feeling sort of blue, because he
suggested we drop by the Swap Sack tonight. Since he never
does this on a weeknight, I wasn't surprised when he explained

on the way over that he knew things were hard for me right now, and that he was going to miss me like crazy, even if we were only going to be apart for two days.

I said, "Please change your mind and come, or at least let me stay here with you and we can fly out together. Haven't you guys noticed all this attention Cara's getting isn't making her any better? If anything, she's getting worse—and now she's practically ruined Christmas."

"Mom got the tickets already," he said, but his voice was thoughtful, as if he saw some merit to what I said. "And I think a change of scenery might not be a bad thing."

Of course, this is the awesome thing about my dad. He always listens carefully to what people say, and even if he doesn't agree, he at least tells them he thinks he understands what they're feeling. Unfortunately, that was the moment when we pulled up in front of the Swap Sack, so the discussion ended. I waited for him to bring up the subject again once we were inside, or after we had collected our usual two bags of books, or while we were having the hot chocolate on the way home, but he didn't.

We listened to Christmas carols on the radio during the drive back, then parked in the driveway and walked up to the front of the house with bags of books in our arms. Little silvery puffs of breath were the only thing coming out of our mouths.

Posted 12/23 @ 3:45 PM

Congrats 4 Chats 3

I feel so sorry 4 u! Even tho I'm heartbroken abut Zeb I think u have it worse, nd all bcuz of ur stupid sister. <long-distance pat on back> It wud b rilly cool if I culd meet u in Seattle, but my dad sez no way. Hang in there, girlfriend!
Posted 12/23 @ 4:00 PM by zo4u

That wud b kool if we all met up. We mite have 2 go 2 tennis camp again nd make sure we're there the same weeks this time. Being a kid sucks sumtimes. I wish there wuz sum way to make ur life btr—I wud email ur sis nd tell her she is a spoiled brat, but that prolly won't help.
Posted 12/23 @ 6:07 PM by tennytrish

Hey, u kno Kyle thot ur dad looked a little sad in church last week, so mebbe it is rilly hard on him, 2.
Posted 12/23 @ 7:09 PM by zbest

Monday, December 28

We're finally back home, and I can't believe how totally awful the trip was—not to mention that my mom's parents are really old and don't even have a computer. Miss Cara was like the princess of the world, getting every drop of attention available, especially when she ate about three bites of food per day.

"Oh, honey, won't you eat something for me?" Grandma would ask her, since you know how grandmas believe food is the way you show your love for your grandkids.

Cara shook her skeleton head "no" sadly and stared at every bite

I took. I'm sure her mental calculator was tallying up the calories.

I hate her. I hate her, I hate her, I hate her! If she was going to ruin my life by being too perfect before, now she's going to ruin it by being perfectly messed up. Mom just pretended like there was nothing wrong, and Dad spent a lot of time talking to Grandma and Grandpa about their funeral. For some reason they're obsessed with dying, but I wanted to say *Excuse me, is this really Christmas kind of stuff?* We hardly ever see them, so I tried to be nice, but it was hard. (Note: Mrs. B never talks about dying or anything like that—props for her. I got her some fresh salmon from the market, and she was thrilled with it.)

But, of course, wouldn't you know, one night at the grandparents' I came downstairs to get a drink of milk and her Highness was there in the kitchen, standing in front of the open refrigerator and stuffing food in her mouth as fast as she could: a slice of cheese, a handful of grapes, two pieces of bread, and who knows what else she would have eaten if I didn't clear my throat to let her know I was there and push past her to get the milk carton.

It was empty.

"You make me sick," I said, and before she could say anything, I went back upstairs and tried not to think about how much she has ruined my life.
Posted 12/28 @ 4:56 PM

Congrats 4 Chats 3

Hey im so glad ur back. itz so good 2 hear from u again, u r like

101

my VBF 2. Not many people r dedicated bloggers like u r, but it rilly is like having a real-time friend nd talking evry day. My Xmas was the same as Thanksgiving: mass confusion, but u made me appreciate that it culd be worse. Happy New Year, at least!
Posted 12/28 @ 5:05 PM by tennytrish

Second that. My evil sister wuz just awful becuz she dint get the ipod she wanted 4 Xmas. She actually pulled down the Xmas tree—can u believe it? I got lots of clothes nd a new cell phone so I wuz rilly happy until she had her tantrum. Mebbe we culd ship her nd Cara off to a desert island sumwhere nd we can 4get they exist.
Posted 12/28 @ 6:07 PM by zo4u

Kyle kept asking me how u were doing the whole time u were gone. He rilly cares abut u nd knos we r such good frenz. In fact, I wuz wondering if u guyz wud let him post here. Just a thot.
Posted 12/28 @ 7:11 PM by zbest

Monday, January 4

Luckily, New Year's wasn't a complete bust like Christmas. I got to sleep over with Maritza and Jess, and that was too fun, for a change. We watched movies all night and ate every kind of left-over Christmas cookie you can imagine. It was such a relief to be with normal girls who enjoy food.

My first day back was as first days usually are, depressing when your teachers load you up with work but thrilling when you see your crush. Jeremy got a haircut over break, and if it's possible, he looks even better!

But then when I walked out of school today, there was Mrs. B in her fur coat, puffing away on a cigarette.

"Megan!" she called, gesturing me over with spirals of smoke following her every move. It wasn't a good time to point out that she was standing in a *smoke-free* zone, since she was clearly excited. Kids on either side of her parted to make sure they didn't walk anywhere near her—not because of the smoke, but because she looked weird.

After I recovered from the embarrassment, it occurred to me to wonder why in the world she might be standing outside the main exit of my school at 3 o'clock in the afternoon. My heart started this crazy-mad pounding then, and the trembly feeling swelled up in my throat. Something must be wrong with Cara.

"What happened?" I asked, but she just shooed me to her car.

Since she got out of the hospital, Mom's been driving Cara to school every day because her backpack is *so heavy*. I (with an equally heavy backpack) still ride the bus (15 minutes of extra sleep), so I didn't even know if she was in school most days, and that's fine with me.

"Your sister is very sick again," Mrs. B said, pulling out of the handicapped spot she'd parked in illegally. "She's at the hospital, and your parents want me to bring you there."

"Is she . . ." I couldn't say the words.

"No, no, she is okay, just very sick with this problem," Mrs. B said, frowning. Here was someone who recognized, like me, that Cara was creating serious issues for my family.

Mom, Dad, and Cara were in the emergency room, the same one they brought me to when I broke my arm. Laying on the stretcher bed, Cara seemed to have shrunk down to the size of a ten-year-old. Her skin was nearly as pale as the sheets.

"Cara called Mom at work today because she thought her heart was racing," Dad explained in the hallway when he and I went to get dinner at the hospital cafeteria. He bit his lip a little, like he does when he's really worried.

"She'll be okay, Dad," I said, looping my arm through his. There was no reason to think this was the truth, but it made him smile and pat my hand.

"You're a good girl, Eggy," he told me.

Two hours later, Cara was admitted to the same floor she'd been on before, but Dr. M told Mom and Dad she really needed to go to a hospital where they specialize in eating disorders. That made me like him even less—wasn't _he_ a doctor? Shouldn't he be able to help people, not make them cry like Mom was doing?

"The place I recommend is in <u>Arizona</u>," Dr. M continued, and he might as well have said <u>Europe</u> or a foreign country, because I know Arizona is nearly as far away as <u>California</u>, but, rumor has it, not nearly as pretty.

You can imagine how our house has been since we left the hospital. Awful:

1. Mom was so hysterical that Dad called <u>her</u> doctor, who happens to go to our church. He brought some medicine for Mom right to our house—how often does that happen?

2. Dad told me he was going to pray for Cara to get better so she wouldn't have to go to Arizona and asked if I wanted to join him. I knew he would be disappointed if I didn't, but honestly, I've had it with Cara. All she needs to do is eat and this whole drama will end. What is wrong with her? Luckily, Dad went with silent prayer, so I mentally organized my homework and then slipped away to do it once he said *Amen* out loud.

3. When I IM'd Mark's screen name it bounced back to me—what gives?

4. Because of 1, 2, and 3, I cried myself to sleep.
Posted 1/4 @ 11:34 PM

Congrats 2 Chats 2

Oh sweet 1, how can this get ne worse? <many, many mental hugs>
Posted 1/4 @ 11:45 PM by zo4u

Sorry my mom caught me on the cellphone nd made me hang up. u get the message, tho, this is just 2 much 4 a grl our age 2 deal /w! Mrs. B sounz like the most norml 1—mebbe she can clue ur parents in.
Posted 1/4 @ 11:58 PM by zbest

Monday, January 11

Well, it's official: Cara is in Arizona. Everything happened so quickly, but I guess that's what she wanted: to get away from us. As soon as she found out she was going there, she went online and then made Mom take her shopping for a bunch of new clothes. How weird is that? There's something just wrong and sick with making your heartbroken mother take you out shopping the morning before you fly across the country to be admitted to a hospital. (At this point, they must have gone to the preteen section since I don't think Cara is even eating secret snacks anymore.)

Mom took her to Arizona, and when they left for the airport, Cara actually seemed excited and not at all sad to be leaving Dad and me.

Dad is really tense, and so they brought the previous pastor, Pastor Ken, out of retirement to *help out* at the church. I can only imagine the terrible things everyone is saying.

And who is our staunchest defender? Mrs. B. She makes Dad cookies and tells him not to worry about the *church clique* because they're just a bunch of bored old ladies. (She should know—she used to be their ringleader! Now I guess she thinks we can't function without her, and she might be right. I know she is my reliable source of excellent food and interesting stories!)

Even AAP is dragging a bit. Last week I started and threw away three new drawings because they kept morphing into Cara-like girls on a journey somewhere. Over break, I finished the one collage piece I liked a lot, but then when I showed it to Mr. Walker it suddenly looked like something a fourth grader might make. Mr. Walker said, "Not bad," but I didn't believe him.

Today when I was waiting for Dad to pick me up after AAP, Jeremy walked out with his portfolio tucked under one arm and a backpack dangling from the other. As usual, he looked sort of dreamy and not aware of anything around him until I said, "Hey."

"Oh, Megan, hey. I didn't expect to see you here—where's your sidekick in the fur coat?" he asked.

"Mrs. B had a doctor's appointment, so my dad's coming today," I said, looking straight ahead and wishing I hadn't said anything, because I knew what was coming next.

"I heard about your sister," he said, as I thought he would. "Man, Arizona, that's really far away. How's she doing?"

Hello! She's in a hospital, surrounded by doctors and nurses whose life mission is to take care of girls like her. Last night when she called they were doing equine therapy, which means they go out and ride horses. Does that sound like someone in distress to you? No one has asked Dad or Mom or me how we're doing, and we're the ones who are still here, trying to pretend nothing's wrong.

I take it back. Mrs. B asks how we all are every time she sees us, then takes a long drag of her cigarette, shakes her head in that Mrs. B kind of sorrowful way, and tells me to *persevere.* I guess she should know about hard times because she was in a concentration camp during World War II, though she doesn't remember any of it because she was a baby. She grew up without a mom or dad since they both got killed for helping Jews get out of Europe. How can I feel bad about my life?

Both of my grandmas have called, and after the quickest "Hi, Eggy" they ask for Dad or Mom, and I can tell the first thing they say is "How's Cara?" Typical.

Dad pulled up before I could give a good answer to Jeremy's question, so I just said good-bye and got in the car. Maybe I slammed the door a little too hard.

Lisa, I forgot all about Kyle. I don't know—this is sort of a bad time in my life to start sharing personal things with someone new, but maybe he would have some good ideas?
Posted 1/11 @ 4:57 PM

Congrats 4 Chats 3

I dunt kno if a guy wud be helpful, especially 1 we dunt kno that well. Ur call, eggs! I kno how u feel nd it sukz. My sister has now decided to run away again, so my parents hired sum detective to go downtown nd look 4 her like they did last time . . . nd the time b4. If she doesn't like it here, why duznt she find sum place better nd stay there?
Posted 1/11 @ 5:10 PM by zo4u

If I was in California we could have a real sob fest right now, how about it? Do you ever walk down the hallway at school and look at all the *normal* girls and wish you could be like them, nothing really exciting happening in your life, but nothing terrible either? I wrote Mark a letter since the screen name won't work.
Posted 1/11 @ 5:31 PM by sistrsic92

I think Kyle is trying 2 b helpful, I kno it mebbe felt like he wuz snooping or sumthing . . . but hez rilly gr8, nd he duz understand bcuz of his cousin. Btw, I met her over break, nd she went to that same place in Arizona. She sez it's rilly a good place.
Posted 1/11 @ 5:45 PM by zbest

Monday, January 25

Today Mom announced that we are all flying to Arizona for something called "Family Week" at Cara's hospital. It sounds too much like <u>Family Therapy</u> to me, so I refused to go. That shocked both Mom and Dad, since I always go along with what they want.

"Eggy, we're a family, we have to go together," Mom said with the really sad face she puts on when I disappoint her.

"I'm tired of being a family with Cara. She didn't have any problem leaving <u>us</u>! And don't you care about my life at all? This is a really important time in AAP, and I'll have to miss two sessions!" I didn't add that she hadn't even looked at the collage I had spread all over the dining-room table, or that Mrs. B and Jeremy have given me more encouragement with my art than she has.

"Megan Marie, I can't believe you'd say something like that! Your sister is very sick, and we all need to do everything we can for her," Mom said before Dad could try and play peacemaker like he usually does. What a guiltfest—I couldn't stand to look at either of them for one more minute, so I ran upstairs with Casper and shut myself in my room.

There was a razor blade lying on my desk because I had been cutting pictures out of a magazine to make a collage for Cara, and before I could stop myself, I picked it up and cut a gash in my leg. It really hurt, but there wasn't even that much blood, like you might think from those slasher movies.

I don't know why I did it, maybe because it's such a big deal at our school like everywhere else in the world that teenage girls exist. Last year we had a whole health class on it, and how girls use cutting as a *coping mechanism* (think typical adult attempt to act like they understand teenagers), but that's not how it was for me—I was just so mad at everyone. After a couple of seconds it did start to bleed and I got a little woozy just looking at it. Then came the pain.

The sad thing is, neither Dad or Mom came up to check on me after our fight downstairs. I guess they thought they were giving me *space* (see above) or maybe the phone ringing was Cara calling from Arizona. Whenever she calls, we all put our lives on hold to listen to her talk about the food they're forcing her to eat in Arizona. At least Casper seems to care that I was upset—he has what I call HSP—human sensory perception.

One time, in the locker room, Jess told me she used to cut herself—since no one but my blog pals will ever read this, I can write that without violating a confidence. She still has scars on her arms from it, but pretty high up so they're hard to see. Her life is so perfect compared to mine I couldn't understand why she would ever want to do something like that, but she said her mom puts a lot of pressure on her as the only daughter.

"Did you get caught?" I'd asked her, because if I saw the marks so easily in gym class, surely everyone at home did.

"No," she said with this sort of strange, satisfied smile that made me wonder if she really had stopped like she said.

Part of me wanted to play reporter and ask a million more questions, but part of me said don't bother because I'm not even Jess's VBF, so why would she confide in me?

Speaking of Jess, yesterday she freaked out on me. We were eating lunch and all I did was ask Jess how things were going with her brothers. "What do you mean?" she asked in this shrill voice. Normally she would jump right in and complain like crazy about them hacking into her website or eating her dessert when she wasn't looking, but for some reason, she stared at me like my face had just turned to rubber. Maritza stopped chewing her food and frowned at both of us.

"Well, you know," I said kind of lame, "sometimes they don't treat you real well."

"Oh, and look who's talking! Ms. 'I have to go to Arizona for a week because my sister has an eating disorder,'" Jess answered, kind of flipping her hair back in that way that lets me know she thinks I'm incredibly stupid.

"Hey, Jess, lay off," Maritza told her when she saw my

eyes getting kind of wet.

As you can imagine, Maritza defending me only made Jess madder. When lunch was done, she stomped out of the cafeteria ahead of me and Maritza, who had meanwhile launched into a big debate about whether I should send Mark the old-fashioned handwritten letter I wrote him or forget him for good and launch a full-scale attack to win Jeremy's affections.
Posted 1/25 @ 7:34 PM

Congrats o Chats 5

<sounds of commiseration> BTDT, friend. But if ur rents find out that you cut urself, u kno they will go nuts nd you'll b the next person in the hospital, so b careful! I confess I tried cutting only once but I am a real coward when it comz 2 pain.

Neway, dunt u think thaz kinda weird that we wud hurt urselves more when we r already hurt? I'm not into ur sister's way of coping (food) nd I'm too paranoid 2 do drugs, so that leaves my guitar. Now I just go up nd play like crazy as u can tell frm the music on my blog. Here's the weird thing, tho—if I sumday get a big record contract I can personally thank my sister 4 all the crap she put me thru bcuz otherwise I wudnt have known I culd be musical!
Posted 1/25 @ 8:02 PM by zo4u

Megan, u rilly need 2 level /w ur parents. Mebbe u culd go away 2 skool or sumthing—thats wut 1 of my friends did 2 get away from a sick sister (worse than urs, believe it or not). U dunt want 2 ruin ur life, 2.
Posted 1/25 @ 8:30 PM by tennytrish

I wonder if I could pretend to fly to Phoenix and then hitchhike to California and live with one of you. Zoey, since your sister ran away, would your parents mind? They sound way cooler than mine, and if we both are missing a sister, we can have each other. What do you think?
Posted 1/25 @ 8:45 PM by sistrsic92

That wud b so cool! Letz do it, they will never even kno bcuz my room is such a mess twenty ppl culd live there nd no 1 wud guess. . . .
Posted 1/25 @ 9:00 PM by zo4u

B real, u 2. Hitchhiking is so dangerous! Mebbe u culd stay /w me since ur parents kno mine from church? I can ask. U nd me nd Kyle culd hang out nd do whatever u want.
Posted 1/25 @ 9:24 PM by zbest

Wednesday, January 27
Here I am in Arizona, using the hotel's computer in the main lobby where anyone can see, and some weird dude keeps watching me, so this will be quick. Clearly, Mom and Dad got their way, and I'm off to Family Week.

"Think of it as a vacation!" Mom had said, which is so typical of her trying to make the best of everything—I'm surprised she didn't wrap up some gift baskets to bring along.

My leg is still sore from where I cut it, and one time I came close to doing it again, but every time I take a shower it just kills to have water on it in the first place so I haven't. Brought my sketchbook and am trying to do a lot of art (like Zoey and her music), as well as bury my nose in a book, but I'm having trouble focusing.

The thing is, I don't really want to miss school for any kind of pseudo Family Week, and AAP is the one place I feel safe and accepted for who I am. Yesterday, before we left, I was waiting inside the front doors for Mrs. B when Jeremy came up and leaned against the wall next to me.

"Hey, I heard you tell Mr. Walker about going away," he said.

"Yeah, for a whole week." I just kept staring straight ahead so I wouldn't look into his soft brown eyes and melt completely. "To visit my sister in the hospital."

"Bummer." He was quiet for a moment, then he took a big breath in and shoved his hands deep in his pockets. "You know, I've actually been in almost the same situation myself."

I was so surprised I did look at him then. His face was completely honest, but I think it was hard for him to go on.

"It's my mom. She's schizophrenic, and I've spent about as much time visiting her in hospitals as I've spent with her at home."

"Oh, Jeremy, I'm sorry," I said, but then I couldn't think of anything else to say. It was horrible, because I really wanted to be comforting, but having a sick mom for most of your life is just too awful to imagine.

He told me there had been a lot of problems with his mom until she went to live with her family in Florida a few years ago. I guess she might have done some terrible things to him, because

115

it doesn't sound like he wants to see her again, but his dad forces him to visit her once a year.

So, now at least one other person might understand how I feel. I almost told him about this blog, but then I decided not to since all that stuff about Mark and Jess and cutting is in here. (Speaking of whom, Mark <u>still</u> hasn't answered the letter—I decided to send it. . . .) Anyway, it's like the four of us are VBFs already, and to be honest, Kyle and Lisa and I have been hanging around in youth group, and I wonder if she isn't right about letting him be part of my blog. (He swore he would keep it an absolute secret.)

Arizona sure is a lot of desert, and we're not even to the place where Cara is staying—I guess we have to drive a lot further. Mom keeps bugging me to come and swim with her and Dad in the hotel pool, but of course the second I put on a bathing suit they'll see my leg and know what's been going on, so I just laid on a deck chair and read.

I doubt I'll be able to write again until I get back . . . and you may not want to know what happens.
Posted 1/27 @ 11:36 AM

Congrats 2 Chats 1

Oh sweetie, I'm sorry they're making u do this. Of course, my house isn't the best rite now, either, bcuz they found my sister at the same place they find her every other time she ran away (her ex-boyfriend's loser cousin's house). My rents r majorly pissed at her because the police sed next time they'll do more than just bring her home.

Good news on the horizon 4 urs truly, though. Met a new guy at school—literally he just moved here frm Michigan, nd guess wut—he's a drummer. We jammed a little bit in my garage this weekend, nd if I do say so myself, we're not bad. Culd a famous band b in the future?

Keep ur chin up! <sounds of encouragement>
Posted 1/27 @ 3:44 PM by zo4u

Wednesday, February 3

Do I want to remember or forget the details of *Family Week*?
First off, if you ever get an eating disorder, you should definitely
head for the place where Cara is. It's gorgeous, with a swimming
pool and everything you would need to get better. Of course, who
wouldn't want to stay someplace like that as long as possible when
they have a dance studio and an art studio and horseback riding?

But that's the upside.

The downside is that you're stuck there with other girls who are
obsessed—and I mean <u>obsessed</u>—with every calorie that goes into
their mouths. Now I understand why Cara goes on and on about
what she's eaten (or refused) every time she calls home. These
people are like walking food dictionaries, and after a while I just
wanted them all to shut up about carbs and proteins and fats and
whatever else it is that they keep track of in those mental registers
of theirs. (Lisa, your teacher's control theory was right on!)

"How does this work?" I asked Dad at one point. "You take a bunch of girls who are sick because of food and put them some-place where they can only think and talk about food?" Even the art they do is about food!

Dad nodded his head like he does when we have a secret agreement. "I'm with you on that one, Eggy, but your sister does look better."

Truthfully, she did. They must have made her gain weight because she had some of her old figure back, and for the first time in a long time she actually looked happy. She made me a mirror with funny stickers and feathers all around it and took me around and introduced me to all the other girls she was friends with, which made me feel like I at least mattered to her. When I gave her a collage I made in AAP especially for her, she put it up on the bulletin board over her bed, right next to a picture of our family from last Christmas.

We had to sit through <u>hours</u> of therapy, but it wasn't as bad as Dr. M, and when it came to Cara she told us she realized she has a great family and that it wasn't our fault she got an eating disorder. Everyone clapped, and she hugged each of us and said she loved us, but it made me wonder: if we're not the problem, then what is?

The therapist says if things keep going well, Cara can come home in another two weeks, but she'll have to go to therapy a lot and keep working on her *nutritional intake.* That shouldn't be a problem, since I know she is already obsessed with food.

But if you're thinking about moving to Arizona or even taking a trip there, in a word, DON'T! First off, once you leave the city parts, you have to drive forever to reach another city or little town. Second, it's wicked hot, like when you open the oven door and a blast of heat comes out at you. Mom told me a lot of people like Arizona for that reason, but here's one person who doesn't. Who wants to feel like their body is being ironed every time they step outside?

Last, the desert is really depressing, just miles and miles of nothing that makes you realize how alone you can be in the world. I didn't tell Dad this, but it reminded me of some of his sermons about people who got stuck in deserts, like Moses and Jesus. Yours truly would be a raving lunatic if someone dropped me off and left me out there all alone for even an hour.
Posted 2/3 @ 7:18 PM

Congrats 4 Chats 5

<sounds of laughter> ur 2 fune. We go 2 Las Vegas a lot nd that means driving thru lots of desert, but I like it becuz where I live there's 2 much of evrythin nd u feel stressed by all the people nd cars nd stuff like that.

Big news—drummer boy (DB) axd me 2 go 2 the movies this weekend. Of course, in addition 2 being thrilled nd saying yes, I made sure my ex knew abut it. Btw, how's ur love life? Hav u talked 2 Jeremy since u got back or heard from Mark?
Posted 2/3 @ 8:56 PM by zo4u

Welcome back! I missed not reading ur blog. It wuz weird, I almost called u on my cell but my rents are like urs abut long distance nd text messaging. I'm like the only girl in my grade who

can't text, thanks 2 my mom hearing a story at work abut sum kid who ran up a $200 bill one time!
Posted 2/3 @ 9:23 PM by tennytrish

Hey guyz, Megan sed I hafta ax u 2 abut letting Kyle post on here. He rilly iz a good guy but if u don't want 2, I understand.
Posted 2/3 @ 10:17 PM by zbest

Itz Megan's blog. If she sez itz okay, thaz okay by me.
Posted 2/3 @ 10:30 PM by zo4u

Mebbe. U can always block him if it duznt work out.
Posted 2/3 @ 10:40 PM by tennytrish

Monday, February 15

Well, it's <u>Valentine's Day</u> (at school anyway), and the only thing I got was a heart-shaped tart from Mrs. B, so that should tell you the status of my romantic relationships. Good for you, Zoey! See, it's just like we told you, someone else did snag you after your big breakup because you are such a good person. That's what VBFs are for!

Jeremy passed me in the hallway today but said absolutely nothing, even though I'm sure he saw me. Maybe he feels weird about what he told me about his mom?

Trip came up to me at lunch and said, "So, what's wrong with Cara? Is she like, hurling all the time?" He made this barf noise, and his friends, who were standing behind him, laughed really loud, which provided me with the perfect moment of mortification since everyone at the nearby tables turned to look at us. It was only a moment, though, because an amazing thing happened. Maritza stood up and got right in his face.

"You're not funny, Todd. In fact, you are *asqueroso sumo puerco*! Girls wouldn't even get eating disorders if guys like you didn't talk about boobs and butts all the time!"

You wouldn't believe it. Trip kind of shrank down and actually looked embarrassed. "Whatever," he said, and he and his posse left to torment some other poor soul.

"I can't believe you said that," I told Maritza as soon as they were out of hearing range. "Thank you. By the way, what did it mean?"

"Extremely disgusting pig," she said, staring after him with hard eyes. "My brothers would never treat a girl like that."

So now I have a new champion, which means I actually have two champions, since Jess does whatever Maritza does and vice versa. The two of them went to the principal together and reported Trip! I didn't know anything about it until my guidance counselor called me in and asked if I needed to talk about anything.

I wanted to say, "No, thank you, I've just had about two hundred hours of therapy thanks to my sick sister, and I feel worse instead of better."

What I really said was, "I'm fine."

Tomorrow is AAP. I wish Jeremy would talk to me, but if he's like me, giving out really personal information like that can be a little scary. You never know if the other person will broadcast it around school. (In the case of Jess, you can count on that exact thing happening.)

Mark and I have started IMing (he's alive, with a new screen name!). He said he was *seeing someone* but there's still hope, I think, since they have *issues* (welcome to my world). Here's part of what we said last night:

sistrsic: so do you have a GF now

Tenman: yeah, I do

Tenman: we met when I came back to school

sistrsic: that's nice, I guess

Tenman: sometimes

Tenman: sorry, have bad case of pos tonite, have 2 keep shutting down brb

Tenman: locked in br with laptop—only way to get privacy in my house

sistrsic: does your GF play tennis too

Tenman: badly

sistrsic: not as bad as me, I hope

Tenman: close ☺

Tenman: you tried the hardest of anyone at camp. I admired that

sistrsic: you were nice to me when I sucked at tennis. I admired that

Tenman: u r cute

sistrsic: ditto

Tenman: have to go or my sister will break down the door. Ttyl

So despite the hundreds of miles between us, there is hope!
Posted 2/15 @ 8:39 PM

Congrats 4 Chats 3

♥ from me 2 u! nd the same 4 zbest ♥
Posted 2/15 @ 8:49 PM by zo4u

♥ ♥ 2 u both, 2. dunt worry, Megan, I dint get nething at all . . . unless u count a heart-shaped cookie from my mom.
Posted 2/15 @ 8:55 PM by tennytrish

Kyle here. Thanks for letting me post! I am *greatly honored* to be the only guy!
Posted 2/15 @ 9:47 PM by kyleawhile

CHAPTER 16

Saturday, February 20

Cara came home today, and although I am still so mad at her for ruining our family, I <u>was</u> glad to see her. At first she was kind of down because the newspaper had an article about the girls' swim team getting ready for finals, which Cara won't be a part of, obviously. Back when she and Tonya were still friends, they couldn't stop talking about breaking all the school swim records before they graduated.

Mom was there, though, and kind of folded up the paper and suggested we might go to the mall and buy a few clothes for school, since the ones Cara has don't fit anymore. Cara brightened up right away. I guess now she must be a size 2 instead of a size 0.

Mom dropped us off because I think she thought some *together time* would help our sisterly relationship. We had so much fun I almost forgot that 24 hours ago she was in a hospital for girls with major problems. While we ate pizza, she told me about a lot of the people she met there and laughed at some of the stupid activities they had to do.

"Eggy, you wouldn't believe it, they made us pretend to be an animal that expressed our feelings, so there were all these girls"—she laughed so hard she had to stop for a second—"all these girls crawling around on the floor or pretending they could fly. It was hilarious."

It sounded stupid to me, but I laughed so she would think I agreed with her. "What animal were you?"

"I was a bear," she said, "big and fat and hibernating in a cave."

"Calla, you're not fat!"

The smile went completely off her face, and she got up and walked away so fast I had to hurry to catch up with her.

"What's the matter?" I asked. "It's true, you're not fat!"

"I am too, Eggy. They made me gain weight so I'd be fat. Look at this flab." She grabbed the side of her thigh and shook it. "Now Mom and Dad are going to bug me to gain even more until I look like a fat pig."

"Calla, that's muscle. You have a lot of muscle from swimming and field hockey." As soon as I said it, I felt bad for reminding her in any way that she was going to be missing one of the highlights of her senior year.

"What do you know, Eggy? You're just a kid."

Thankfully, that was the only dark moment of the evening. We had ice cream on the way home, which I dutifully reported to Mom later when she grilled me about it. I still think it's weird to call yourself fat when you weigh less than 100 pounds.
Posted 2/20 @ 11:30 PM

Congrats 2 Chats 4

If I can give u sum advice it wud b this, just ignore ur sistr's weird behavior bcuz u can't change it, no one can. My sic sistr tries 2 get me mad at my rents all the time bcuz she thinx they r so mean. granted, they can be typical rents but they don't beat us or nething like that. <eyes filling /w tears>

On a happier note, the movie was so fun nd we ran into sum of my other friends who r musical types nd just came back to my house nd hung out all nite. DB plays a bunch of instruments nd knoz everything there is to know about music—he downloaded some alternative stuff 4 me nd I rilly like it. I like him too.
Posted 2/20 @ 11:45 PM by zo4u

Cara still rocks as a swimmer. Your school swims against mine, and she set a record here last year, in butterfly no less. It's not my *personal preference* but she can really nail it. I'm a back-stroker, but I didn't make finals.
Posted 2/20 @ 11:53 PM by kyleawhile

Hey, Kyle, welcome!
Posted 2/20 @ 11:54 PM by zo4u

Ditto.
Posted 2/20 @ 11:58 PM by tennytrish

Monday, February 22

I know Cara got a lot of attention back at school today because her lunch table was packed and everyone was talking to her. (Except for Trip, who kept his distance.) I tried not to stare, but she looked so pretty and happy in spite of her thinness, I couldn't help breathing a sigh of relief. The whole Arizona deal might have been weird and expensive, but it worked, and now that she's better, hopefully life will get back to normal.

Not everyone was happy, though. We had AAP today, and no matter what Mr. Walker said, Jeremy mumbled and kept to himself, which gave me the signal that I should leave him alone. It wasn't one of the more fun sessions we've had. Usually those of us who draw tend to stick together and help each other out, but everyone was quiet and maybe a little tense because we only have about two months left to finish our projects.

My pictures suddenly seemed to suck big time to me—what was I thinking by even trying AAP? Maritza had this idea for me to take some random photos and use pieces of them in my collages, but they looked stupid or maybe I'm just a bad photographer.

When we were done, I followed Jeremy out the door, far enough behind so he could talk if he wanted to, but not so close that he would think I was stalking him. Just as we were near the lobby, who should come around the corner but Trip and his gang.

When Casper sees something interesting in the distance (usually

128

a squirrel), his ears perk up and he comes to full attention before he dashes toward it. That's exactly how Trip looked when he saw Jeremy, but only for a second. Then he charged at him and slammed him back against the lockers.

"Don't you ever blab on me again, faggot," he said, grabbing Jeremy's shirt and twisting it tight around his neck.

Just as quick, he punched Jeremy hard in the stomach, but before he could do anything more, he saw me coming toward them and let go. Jeremy slumped to the floor, and Trip gave me this *I dare you to do something* look.

I could have walked by or turned around and headed in the other direction. I could have gone back and told Mr. Walker. Instead, I somehow found the courage to walk right up to Trip. "What is wrong with you, Trip?" I yelled at him. "Why do you have to be so mean?" My voice was shaking because I wouldn't put it past Trip to hit me, too, but more than that I was mad at him for the way he treated Cara and me and now Jeremy.

Trip gave one of those snorting little laughs through his nose and repeated what I said in this fake falsetto voice. Then he walked away with his other guy friends who, for once, didn't say a word.

"Are you okay? Should I go find a teacher?" I asked Jeremy, kneeling down so we were eye to eye.

He was leaning forward with both arms across his stomach, so I know he was in pain, but before he could answer, Mr. Walker came strolling down the hall with his backpack in one hand and his car keys in the other. When he saw me and Jeremy, he rushed over.

"What's going on here?" he asked in that stern teacherly voice they all use to exert authority.

"Nothing. I'm okay," Jeremy said weakly. "I've had the flu, and my stomach still hurts a little. I felt like I had to sit down for a minute, but I'm okay now."

Mr. Walker looked at me for confirmation, but I looked away. It wasn't my place to squeal on Trip—and that might get Jeremy in more trouble.

"We better give your dad a call to come get you," Mr. Walker said, suspicious.

Jeremy was slowly sliding up into standing position, his back still against the lockers. The color was returning to his face, but he kept one hand pressed against his stomach. "Really, I'm okay, Mr. Walker. Thanks for the offer, but I can drive myself home," he said.

"Come on, I want you to sit down for a few minutes so I can make sure you're okay." Mr. Walker, in full authority mode, took Jeremy's arm and led him toward some benches in the lobby. I trailed behind, carrying Jeremy's portfolio and backpack.

"Sit down, and I'll get you a drink of water," Mr. Walker said, pointing to a seat. He had obviously taken lessons from the school nurse on how to deal with *student health crises.*

As soon as I was sure he couldn't hear, I turned back to Jeremy. "Jeremy, why didn't you tell him what happened?" I demanded.

"Because." Jeremy winced and shifted position. "That's why Trip hit me in the first place—for getting him in trouble."

"What do you mean?"

"It's nothing. Don't worry about it." He looked away.

"Jeremy, I know you're in classes with Jess's brother, Charlie, so I can find out if you don't tell me."

Jeremy looked toward the hallway where Mr. Walker had gone to get the water and saw it was still empty.

"Actually, it kind of has to do with Cara," Jeremy said, and I felt my eyes widen. "Trip was making fun of your sister in the locker room yesterday. When I told him to knock it off, he got right in my face and told me I couldn't make him. His timing was bad, though, because the coach just happened to walk in and see what was going on. He really laid into Trip."

Now it was my turn to slump down on the bench next to him, stunned. Before I could think of the right thing to say, Mr. Walker came back.

"Here you go," he announced, holding out a paper cup of water. It was so ridiculous to think a drink of water was going to help Jeremy, but the activity bus pulled up right at that moment, so I had to say a hurried good-bye and dash out the door.

Of course, the first thing I did when I got home was call Jess. She promised to get the full story from Charlie and call me back with all the details.

It makes me feel a little guilty, but I actually forgot about Jeremy because it felt so good to sit down at the table and eat dinner just like we used to, with all four of us as a family, and everyone eating the same things. I didn't even mind when Dad said a longer than usual blessing in thanks for Cara's return.

Jess called back right as I was getting ready to go to bed, her voice excited. "You're not going to believe it, Eggy," she said. I knew then that what she had found out would be extreme, since she rarely uses my pet name for me anymore.

"Spill!" I said.

"Charlie was there when it happened, so he saw the whole thing. I guess Trip has been talking all year about having sex with your sister, and how she kept saying no but he finally got her to give in." Her voice got a little lower. "Charlie said Trip is really gross in the locker room anyway, but I guess today the whole thing got too disgusting. He said he would never want to *screw a skeleton,* and that's when Jeremy told him to knock it off."

I swallowed hard, wondering how much of Charlie's story was true. In the past, he has been known to embellish information with a few spicy details that weren't exactly accurate. Trip's behavior didn't surprise me—but would Cara really have given in to him? She had to know what kind of person he really was, and that would turn any girl off.

"I hate Trip," I said. "He acts so polite and friendly around the teachers so they all think he's wonderful. But when they're not around, he's the total opposite. I'm glad the coach caught him today, but I wish Jeremy didn't get in trouble for it." I paused for a moment, thinking about the night when I saw Cara pushing Trip's hand away from her sweater again and again. "I don't think Cara would ever sleep with him."

"Why don't you ask her what happened and tell her about Jeremy?" Jess suggested.

"I can't right now, Jess. She doesn't need anything more to upset her, but if Trip does one more thing, I'm telling my mom, and then he better look out."

"I hear you on that one," Jess said. "Hey, you owe me big time for the info. I had to promise Charlie I'd get Maritza to go out with him this weekend before he'd spill the beans."

Charlie's ongoing crush on Maritza had been the subject of many sleepover and lunchtime discussions between Jess, Maritza, and me. Given her behavior lately, I thought she might go out with him just to help me, but I wasn't sure our friendship went quite that far.

I sucked my breath in, knowing that if Maritza did go, I would never hear the end of it. "Did you ask her? What did she say?"

"She'll do it, but only because she wants to see if Charlie will tell her anything else. You know, Maritza's gotten a little obsessed with Trip and this whole deal. She won't stop calling him a *pedazo de mierda*, which she says means *piece of shit.* I wish I spoke another language—you can get away with saying things like that in school when the teachers don't know what you mean."

"Yeah, me too. She really hates him. She told me if her dad or her brothers ever heard Trip talk about a woman like he did my sister, they'd make him stop for good." I made a sound of admiration. "I can't believe Maritza stood up to Trip like she did—I think that's what gave me the courage to do it, too. It's not fair that he gets away with being so crude."

We made a plan to discuss everything further this weekend, during a sleepover at my house. Since things with Cara have settled down, I finally felt like I could have Maritza and Jess over like I'd been promising them, and Lisa might come too if she's not with Kyle. It's too exciting—who knows what secrets we'll find out after Maritza has her date with Charlie?
Posted 2/22 @ 10:45 PM

Congrats 1 Chats 2

Imho, ur friend Maritza soundz just like my aunt frm Mexico. Itz rilly true they have different beliefs nd women do get treated /w more respect in sum ways. (they also have 2 wait on men hand nd foot, but thaz another subject.) It is funny when she getz mad at my uncle nd swearz in Spanish—I axd her 2 teach me how! I can't wait to meet Jess nd Maritza . . . I think.
Posted 2/22 @ 11:09 PM by zbest

mucho gusto! thaz abut all the Spanish I kno! I took six years in school nd have gone on exchange trips 2 Mexico but I can barely follow. Ppl speak it so fast nd excited.
Posted 2/22 @ 11:30 PM by zo4u

Saturday, February 27

We all agree that my sleepover was our best ever, although Maritza didn't get any new information from Charlie. (Their *date* was one hour at the pizza shop before she came over to my house with four leftover slices of pepperoni!)

By 11 PM we had eaten two bags of pretzels and a gallon of chocolate chip ice cream and watched the video Lisa brought (sorry Kyle, it was girls only—even Casper got banned from the basement once we settled in). Jess pulled out the latest issue of her favorite fashion magazine, and we decided to do makeovers (again). I seemed to be the candidate most in need of *improvement* (did I mention Lisa is drop-dead gorgeous?), so Maritza pulled out all the makeup and hair stuff she had brought along. She travels with an extra suitcase full of the stuff.

When my sister walked into the basement and saw Jess using the flat iron on my hair, she just rolled her eyes. (She and I are alike

in that way—we don't fuss much with makeup or hair stuff—or at least we haven't.) But if it makes me look so much better, maybe I need to start. I can't decide. It's a LOT of work to sacrifice sleep for in the morning.

I'm not sure if Jeremy is the one I want to impress, though. Mark is still in the picture, and he is so nice that I find myself wondering if he's got better boyfriend potential than Jeremy, who really doesn't seem as interested as Jess thinks he is. Boys are so confusing! Here's the list we made up:

Jeremy
• Older, drives
• Cute and dreamy
• Artistic
• Here

Mark
• Buff and my age
• Could be a male model
• Athletic
• Far away

So there you have it. Lisa says Kyle is a bit of both Mark and Jeremy—how lucky is she? On the surface, Mark is clearly everything a girl could want, and Jeremy is not, or at least not in the traditional ways. The big downside about Mark is that he is hundreds of miles away, so the chances of us connecting face-to-face before tennis camp (I already bugged Mom to sign me up again—she's holding out for some reason) are remote. Still, I've been thinking about joining the tennis team at school so I'll improve by the time June rolls around. My jockette genes must be kicking into action.

All Cara seems to want to do is email and IM some girls she met in Arizona—I hope they're not exchanging calorie counts, but there's something suspicious about having to close your bedroom door just to write an email—like every red-blooded teenager, she knows about the "Minimize" button.

Posted 2/27 @ 4:30 PM

Congrats 3 Chats 5

Jeremy sonz like DB <heavy sigh> Frm my experience, if u r going 2 b involved wit an artist u can 4get abut the hansum prince deal we got in fairy tales, but itz worth it, trust me. DB nd I r now officially a couple, nd we r forming our own band, name tbd. Ne ideas?

Posted 2/27 @ 4:45 PM by zo4u

How about ther4u, because that really describes how you are, and I'm sure it's true of DB. you can be there 4 evry1 musically as well.

Posted 2/27 @ 4:47 PM by sistrsic92

<sound of cheering> u r brilliant!
Posted 2/27 @ 5:51 PM by zo4u

Sorry—I wuz out afc. I still can't blieve wut Trip did. He is bad newz nd will get wut he deserves sumday. Just b careful /w Mark!
Posted 2/27 @ 7:56 PM by zbest

Guyz need to have sleepovers like girls do. Me and my buds have LAN parties, where we all hook up our computers and play games together until we can barely see straight, but sometimes it actually gets kind of boring.

If you want a *male perspective,* pick Jeremy. Long-distance relationships are really hard to maintain—but they are xciting.
Posted 2/27 @ 8:12 PM by kyleawhile

Monday, February 29

I thought things might <u>finally</u> be getting back to normal, but not so. . . .

When I got home from school today, Mrs. B came over with this incredible fudge cake, and let me tell you, it's basically impossible to have only one piece. Although sometimes she gets on my nerves because she thinks she can drop in randomly and expect that I'll always be so excited to see her, there's no denying that the woman is a good cook and always has a funny story to tell.

She and I were sitting in the kitchen, having a piece of cake (her with the usual glass of wine) when Cara came in to make herself some tea. She saw the cake, and her eyes lit up.

"Yummy! Can I have some?" she asked.

Mrs. B took this as a sign that she had personally brought about a miracle cure and cut a big piece for Cara, who grabbed it and went off to her room. (Despite my mellowing, Cara still thinks Mrs. B is a nosey old woman who needs to *get a life.*)

While I ate my second slice, Mrs. B looked at my latest collage (the photograph attempt) and actually gave me some good suggestions.

"Stay right here," she told me.

She left and then came back with this book of pictures taken by a woman photographer way back when pictures were mostly black-and-white. Then she went back home again and got some of her own photographs (yes, she's talented in that way, too—is there anything she can't do?) and showed me how that style of photos might work for my collage. I got really excited and thought about cutting out pieces of photographs and putting my drawings in, which is a cross between collage and drawing.

Mrs. B was still there when Mom got home, which provided the perfect opportunity for me to make a graceful getaway. As I drifted upstairs, I heard poor Mom going through all the *pleasantries* of being asked how she was doing and so on.

When I reached the landing, still thinking about the cool things I was going to do, I spotted Cara tiptoeing into her bedroom—with the rest of the cake Mrs. B had brought over. She gave me this guilty look, then winked and put one finger to her lips as a signal for me not to say anything. No big deal—it had been so long since I saw her eat normally, it was a relief that her appetite returned—and I know that cake is just about irresistible.

When Dad got home, we all (Cara included) ate a huge plate of spaghetti and Mom's famous Salad Soup (lettuce drowning in dressing). It was a good moment, just like when you open your birthday presents and find out you got everything you wanted. Dad laid down his fork, patted his mouth with his napkin, and looked around hopefully.

"I saw Mrs. B on the way in, and she said she brought over my favorite fudge cake. Any chance a hardworking guy can snag a piece?" he asked.

I realized the cake plate was still missing, and couldn't help look at Cara, but before I could open my mouth, she did this little laughy thing and rolled her eyes.

"Actually, it was pretty small, Dad, and I'm afraid you're too late. Eggy and me ate it all."

"Really?" he asked, and he smiled when she nodded. "Well, good for you. It's great to see you eating again, sweetie." He gave her shoulder a gentle squeeze, then patted his stomach. "I shouldn't be eating cake anyway."

Mom was listening to all this with her mouth slightly open and her eyes narrowed, like she does when she knows someone isn't telling the truth. Before she could say anything, though, Cara jumped up and carried her plate to the kitchen.

"I have lots of homework," she announced as she headed upstairs.

"I feel like a romantic night doing dishes with your mother," Dad said with a goofy smile. "Go ahead and do whatever you have to do, Eggy."

I made a point of clearing off the table slowly, trying to listen to what they were saying as they washed and dried at the sink, but each time I came in the kitchen, they stopped talking. Even when I started upstairs, I knew they were having some kind of discussion, but only the emotion of their talk came through, not any words. Mom was clearly upset.

Cara was coming out of the bathroom when I got to the top of the stairs, her eyes watery and her cheeks flushed. She went in her bedroom really fast and didn't say a word to me.

That's why I went into the bathroom. I really didn't need to use it, but there was something so suspicious about her behavior that I couldn't help myself. Maybe someday I will be a detective of sorts, because my instinct was right.

I could smell vomit as soon as I walked in. How gross. And there were little bits of spaghetti still floating on top of the water in the toilet. It didn't take a genius to figure out what Cara had done, but I felt like Jeremy must have when Trip punched him in the stomach. I went right to her room and knocked on the door.

"What?" Cara yanked it open and scowled at me.

"You threw up!" I hissed. "You felt well enough to eat all that cake and a big supper, and then you came up here and made yourself sick."

She looked ready to deny it, but then I saw the empty cake plate, which was on the floor next to her bed, and she couldn't come up with an excuse.

"Don't you say a word," she told me, pulling me into her room and closing the door. "Just keep your big mouth shut."

She plopped down on the floor and rested her head against her knees. I realized she was crying and crouched in front of her.

"Cara, you have to tell someone."

"My therapist knows. She's known all along, and she can't stop it."

"What do you mean?"

"I'm bulimic, Megan. Everyone thinks I'm some glamorous girl just wasting away, and I was, but then things changed, and now I stuff everything I can eat into my mouth and then throw it all back up."

I thought about the candy stash and suddenly understood. "But why?"

She rested her head on one shoulder and closed her eyes. "Don't you think if I knew *why,* I would stop it?"

I could understand her, in a way. The cut on my leg had healed, but there was still a mark there.

When we were in Arizona, one of the counselors said something that really impressed me. "Sometimes we do things that are bad for us in an effort to cope with problems," he explained to the family members who were trying to figure out why their daughter had an eating disorder. Maybe he was right—maybe I had cut myself because I was so upset with Mom and Dad or even the situation.

Unfortunately, or perhaps fortunately, it hadn't helped. If cutting made me feel better, I might still be doing it, but I'm not.

Awkwardly, I put my hand over Cara's and told her I was sorry she was so upset and would do anything I could to help her.

"Then don't tell," she said. "It'll just make things worse."

So I didn't.
Posted 2/29 @ 9:15 PM

Tuesday, March 1
Brace yourself . . . this will be a long post.

I've been too depressed to write, now that I know Cara is not only stuffing herself but then throwing up everything she eats. My parents still haven't caught on. If anything, they're thrilled to see her eating, and although they make her go to therapy twice a week, they act like nothing is wrong.

I came downstairs one morning and found the cereal box completely empty, so I decided to have toast instead, but guess what? No bread. When I complained to Mom, she told me it wasn't a big deal and she would go shopping that night. It was a big deal, though, because she had just gone shopping a few days ago, and most of what she bought was gone.

It's terrible to sit at the supper table, knowing every bite Cara takes will come back up as soon as she finishes. Mom and Dad's room is on the first floor, along with their own bathroom, so I don't know how they'll ever find out what's going on. Cara has been careful to clean up after she barfs since the first time I caught her, but that doesn't mean she isn't dashing to the bathroom after every meal.

"I can't take this anymore," I finally told her last night.

We were in her bedroom, and I had just seen her eat two hamburgers, a big salad, and a double serving of French fries, only to dash to the bathroom as soon as supper was over.

"It's not your problem. Let me deal with it my own way," she said. She was at her desk, doing her math homework as if there was nothing wrong.

"It is my problem. There's never any food to eat when I'm hungry, and the bathroom smells like puke."

"You eat too much anyway."

"Are you trying to make me have an eating disorder, too, and get all obsessed with every bite of food that goes in my mouth? Maybe I should go in and throw up now, so you can see what it's like," I said, jumping to my feet with Casper in my arms.

"Calm down." She punched some numbers into her calculator without looking at me. "You always get too emotional. If you're upset about the food, just ask Mom to buy some more. She will."

"But it's dishonest, Cara! You know as well as me that I've told my share of white lies to Mom and Dad, but this is different.

They think everything is fine and that you're getting better. I heard Mom talking to Grams on the phone last night, and she told her she was so relieved you were over your eating disorder."

She threw down her pencil and gave me a hard look. "Everything is <u>fine</u>."

"You've got to be kidding!"

Our voices must have been much louder than usual, and we realized Cara's bedroom door was open a little when Mom called up the stairs, "Is everything okay, girls?"

"Yes, Mom," Cara said, going over and closing it. She sat back down at her desk, then slammed the cover of her book shut and glared at me. "Okay, sit down—there."

She nodded toward her bed, so I settled myself against the pillows with Casper in my lap. Finally, she was going to reassure me that I was being silly, and that in her own way, she was getting better.

"At first I <u>was</u> really starving myself," Cara said, still at her desk and with her back to me. "But then I got so hungry and light-headed I snuck food—mostly candy and junk food like you saw, 'cause it satisfies you pretty quick. I ate it at night when nobody would see me, and it kind of got to be a ritual. I would starve myself all day and then reward myself at night—but I always limited myself to 1,000 calories. . . . But then I started throwing up those, too.

"I couldn't stop it: starve, binge, throw up, then start all over. When Mom and Dad found out, all they focused on was getting me to eat, so I started to eat again, but I just threw up my food instead of the candy and snacks. It tasted so good when I started eating real food again that I couldn't control my intake like before—but when I'm full I feel disgusting. They'd be so mad if they knew what I'm really doing—everyone would." She still didn't turn around.

"Cara, everyone wants to help you," I objected, but part of me thought she might be right.

My feelings about her eating disorder <u>had</u> changed since I saw her binging and knew what happened after. Puking <u>is</u> disgusting, no matter how you look at it.

"Megan, everyone thinks bulimia is gross." Now she faced me, the tears in her eyes quickly spilling onto her cheeks. "All the girls I've met in the hospital told me to keep it a secret, because people are nicer to anorexics than they are to bulimics."

She got up and took a tissue from the box on her bedside table. I didn't know what to say or do, so I just kept my head down and rubbed Casper's belly in a sort of absentminded way. What she said was all jammed up in my head.

Finally, I said, "Cara, it doesn't matter. You can't keep on like this. When you got sick, I went on the Internet and read everything I could find about eating disorders so that I could understand, and to keep on deceiving everyone and making them think you're okay is the <u>worst</u> thing you can do."

"You're wrong. You don't understand anything." She stood up and then collapsed on the floor, sobbing.

147

I pushed Casper aside and slid down next to her, a little uncomfortable, because this was a side of the Too Perfect To Be True Sister I had never seen. Plus, I'm not really good with other people's tears.

"Come on, Cara, let me go get Mom or Dad," I pleaded. "You know Dad is really good at making people feel better, even if you do have to put up with a few prayers."

"No!" She grabbed my wrist really hard and shook it, her face all ugly with crying. "Don't you dare. They'll just find out that—" She choked on her words and grabbed for the tissue box.

"Find out what?" I asked. Now I sounded like I would start crying, which made Casper look anxiously from me to her. "Nothing can be so bad that you can't tell them. They're our <u>parents</u>, Cara."

This would be the moment of *dramatic pause* I learned about in theater class, back when I thought I had a chance of being an actor or . . . well, maybe a set designer. Nothing could've prepared me for what she said next.

"Trip raped me."

She pushed a wad of soggy tissues against her eyes and leaned forward, crying even harder. Casper nudged up against her with a worried look on his face and tried to get her attention by pawing at her leg.

"Stop," I said and hugged him against my chest, my voice shaky because I didn't really know what to say.

It seems like every day in the paper there's some story about a woman being raped, but she's usually just that—a grown woman, not a high school student formerly perfect in every way. It doesn't make it any easier, I know, but I admit I zoned out a lot in health ed when we talked about how to be a *a good listener* if someone you know has been *sexually assaulted.*

It didn't take long for me to get really mad, though.

I moved closer to her and said, "Cara, he is such a jerk. You need to tell someone so he gets what he deserves. He's stupid and cruel and self-centered. You have to." I didn't add that her former best friend was in danger of the same treatment, but it was hard not to. Tonya hadn't called Cara, but I was still hoping she might.

"I can't! He'll just say I wanted to have sex, and then I'll look like a slut. You're right, he is a terrible person. Why do you think I broke up with him? But I still feel dirty, like there's something he put inside me that I can't control or get rid of." She dropped her hands from her eyes and looked at me. Now her face was like a balloon, all puffed up from crying. "I can't believe I even told you about this!"

She shook her head in disgust. Granted, I'm younger than her and a semi-loser, but she knows I would do anything in the world for her.

She grabbed my shoulders. "You can't tell anyone. I'll be so upset if you do. I'll deny it! I'll never trust you again. Promise me, Megan. Promise you won't tell."

I looked at her for a long time. Then, without saying a word, I pushed Casper out of my lap, jumped up, and ran to my room.
Posted 3/1 @ 8:56 PM

Congrats 2 Chats 4

Life just sukz so bad sumtimz I can't stand it. my VBF had a cousin who got raped by her BBF (xcept of course he wuznt her BBF after that) nd it wuz the pitz. Her rents went 2 the police nd everything. It wuz all over school nd she wuz so embarrassed she dropped out or sumthin like that. u dint promise her nething, so mebbe u shud tell—but who? Ur neighbor soundz craze, but I bet she culd give u some advice if u did 1 of thoz *hypothetical* things, pretending itz a grl not ur sis. Wot do u think?
Posted 3/1 @ 9:04 PM by zbest

I dunno . . . Mrs. B wud prolly figure things out if u asked a *hypothetical* question since she soundz shrewd in that way parents r. But think of it, Megan, ur sistr culd die or sumthing, nd Trip committed a crime that no 1 wud eva no abut. . . .
Posted 3/1 @ 9:45 PM by tennytrish

Trip sounds like a world-class jerk. I think you should tell your dad—or if you want to, Lisa or I can say we heard a *rumor.* As a man of the cloth, he'll know what to do.
Posted 3/1 @ 9:58 PM by kyleawhile

My dad says evil is always punished in one way or another, but I don't see that happening. Jess just called and told me Trip is taking Tonya to prom, if you can believe that (she's a bigger traitor than I thought). Thanks for being there for me. I don't know what I would do without you all!

Posted 3/1 @ 9:13 PM by sistrsic92

CHAPTER 19

Thursday, March 3

The deadline for the AAP competition is getting closer, but all I can think about is Cara and Trip. It's so unchristian to say this, but I really want to hurt him like he hurt her—I keep dreaming up ways to humiliate him à la Maritza. (If I told her what he did, she would come up with some doozies.) I haven't done anything, though, because I don't want to make things worse for Cara than they already are.

Anyway, there's nothing bad enough I could do to him, and in the meantime, Cara is getting sicker. Mom finally figured things out. She must have had suspicions after all. Dad was working late last night, so the three of us went out to eat and had a huge (but delicious) meal. When Cara beelined for the bathroom after she was done, Mom followed and heard her throwing up, which led to a major screamfest in the car on the way home. As soon as we got there, Mom called Cara's therapist.

"She says many girls with anorexia turn to bulimia later because they feel like they deprived themselves of so much when they weren't eating," she told me and Dad after she hung up. We followed her into the living room, where Cara was parked in front of the TV, watching (what else?) the food channel.

"Mom, I don't want to talk about it, especially with you," I heard Cara say when Mom marched in with her report. I was using every drop of my mental energy to encourage Mom to keep going with the conversation.

"Cara, something has to change, or you're going to end up back in the hospital. Bulimia can kill you, even more quickly than anorexia. You remember that movie we saw on the Lifetime Channel."

"That was a stupid movie, Mom." Cara stirred more sugar substitute in her tea, refusing to look at Mom or me.

Ever since then, Mom's tried to get Cara not to eat so much, or not to go to the bathroom right after meals, but it hasn't worked. The whole control thing seems more complicated than calories.

This is Mom's busy selling season, but she feels like she has to be home most days when we get off the bus and even picks us up from school sometimes, which means she's not doing as well at work as she used to, when she worked 100 hours a week. She doesn't even make her welcome baskets anymore, and a couple of times I heard her arguing with her boss on the phone about all the time she's taking off. I pretended to play with Casper—he's such a convenient distraction. Sometimes I love him just for that.

Aside: As an update on my love life (which has been so not on my mind given everything that's going on with Cara), Mark broke up with his girlfriend and wants to come and see me during Spring break! Good news if it were any other time of my life, right?

As of now, I haven't figured out how to share Mark's suggestion with my parents, since clearly it's not the best time to have company—especially someone I don't actually know that well.

Could I perhaps pretend Mrs. B is my family, and temporarily relocate there? Possible . . . not likely . . . maybe a really bad idea.
Posted 3/3 @ 7:45 PM

Congrats 4 Chats 0

Friday, March 4

Tonight, after supper, a miracle happened when I was cleaning up the kitchen. No, Cara didn't decide not to throw up everything she had eaten, but the phone did ring, and when I dashed to get it, I was amazed.

"Hey, Megan, I was wondering if you wanted to go to the opening of that new art gallery downtown tomorrow," Jeremy said, not even waiting to make sure it was really me. I guess no one would ever mistake me for Cara in any way.

Knowing he understands in part what I'm going through (and vice versa) makes me feel kind of close to Jeremy, in a nonromantic way, even. And, as I'm discovering with Cara, when you share a secret with someone, it changes your relationship completely.

Odd that there's a secret I share with both that involves Trip. In one way, it makes you closer, because you understand something no one else does: Trip is a bigger creep than I ever thought possible. In another way, it makes you feel dishonest and not quite right, because in this case, the secrets shouldn't exist. Both Jeremy and Cara should rat Trip out.

Finally, I said, "Umm, can I get back to you on that?"

The last thing I wanted was to ask Mom for permission when she was especially upset with Cara, but I did it anyway. Wonder of wonders, she and Dad did say yes when I got them alone later, although I had to go through the whole third degree about Jeremy. Cara happened to walk in when they were grilling me.

"I know what I said before, but Jeremy really is a good guy," she told them. "We were in history class together, and he's one of the few honestly nice people at our school."

Wow, I thought, I can't believe she's sticking up for me.

That shut my parents up, and later on, I went into her room even though she had just turned the light out and was curled up in bed.

"Thanks for the help with Mom and Dad," I whispered, kneeling at the head of her bed.

"It's true, Eggy. He really is a good guy." She scooted over and patted the bed, so I crawled in, just like we used to do when I was little and afraid of the dark. I realized then how much I truly missed the old Cara—even if she had been a T2P2. "Tell me about you and him," she said.

I started at the beginning, being careful not to include anything about the Trip confrontation or his mom or her. Then I added the story about Mark, but by the time I finished, her eyes were shut, and she was breathing in that deep way she does when she's fast asleep.

The light from outside was coming through her windows, so I could still see her face, which made me sad. She was like a scraped-down version of her formerly beautiful self. You could see all the prettiness would still be there if she gained a little weight and her hair got shiny again, the way it used to be.

I kissed her on the cheek before I left, and she sort of smiled, as if maybe she thought I was someone else. Like maybe Trip, when he had been nice to her and trying so hard to make her his girl-friend, he came to our house and called my dad "sir" all the time.

Posted 3/4 @ 10:39 PM

Congrats 2 Chats 4

Sistrs . . . they can make u feel so good nd so bad. <sound of heavy sigh> A date /w Jeremy—how 2 good 2 b true! <u>Send evry detail as soon as u get home!!</u>

Posted 3/4 @ 10:45 PM by zo4u

I second that notion!

Posted 3/4 @ 11:02 PM by tennytrish

Tefw! Mebbe sumtime we can double date—Kyle likes art, too.

Posted 3/4 @ 11:12 PM by zbest

I'm not in AAP though—*kudos* to you, Megan, for making it!
But I do like all kinds of art and maybe you, me, and Lisa can go
on a photo shoot some day. You could bring along Maritza, too—
we *photogs* enjoy comparing cameras, etc.
Posted 3/4 @ 11:23 PM by kyleawhile

Saturday, March 5

We've gone to some strange exhibits through AAP (did I mention the one with chopped-up parts of dolls and mannequins—too weird), but this time Jeremy and I were the youngest people at the gallery, which made us sort of that novelty everyone approves of. The owner kept telling us how happy it made him to have teenagers there and to make sure we brought our friends in (as if any of us would be able to afford the stuff he had to sell!). But it was interesting: pictures of children with layers of paint over some parts of their faces and bodies but not others and then some kind of laquer on top of it all. (My mind was instantly translating this into collage language.) We were hoping to meet the artist, but he wasn't there.

Jeremy seemed to know way more about the pictures and the artist than most everybody there, and he wore a long-sleeved white hoodie that made him look cuter than usual. I couldn't help wondering if I really wanted to see Mark after all; unfortunately I had already made the plans.

Last night, after an initial outright refusal, Mom eventually agreed to drive me to meet Mark halfway at a ski resort so we can spend one day together skiing. (Of course, Mark is an ace at that too, while yours truly has been on the bunny slope once!) It did make me feel guilty when she asked if Jeremy and Mark were both *just guy friends,* as I insisted.

But back to Jeremy.

"Do you think there's such a thing as a collage artist career?" I asked him after we finished looking at the pictures. We were sitting across from each other at the cute coffee shop next door to the art gallery, sipping insanely expensive coffee drinks (he paid).

"Mixed media is really big right now," he said, taking a swallow of his coffee and smacking his lips a little. It was so Casper-like and cute, I could have hugged him on the spot. (Don't tell me dogs can't express their emotions—when I give Casper a treat, his whole face smiles.)

"Yeah, but I'm kind of nervous about the competition. My art is so different than everyone else's, and if it's anything like what we just saw, I'm so out of luck."

He shrugged. "Hey, you're a sophomore. This is my third year of entering, so it's my last chance."

"You'll do fine. You're really talented." Jeremy took another slug of his real coffee (straight up), while I sipped on my fancy flavored drink that cost about three times as much. As soon as I ordered it, I worried that he would think I'm frivolous, especially since Maritza insisted I wear her low-cut top with the nearly see-through material. Mom made me put something on under it, thankfully, since I don't have as much to show off as Maritza.

Still, it was another nice thing Maritza has done for me lately, and it did make me feel sort of pretty. (Aside: Jess has decided to go out for track and is all about the boys on the team. I wonder if our threesome might be pulling apart? Deeper question: Does Maritza really like me—we do have some things in common—or am I just convenient until she finds cooler friends to replace me with?)

Anyway, back to my conversation with Jeremy.

"I've never done a real show before, though, and I'm way behind where I want to be." I hesitated, not sure how personal we were going to get. "Things at my house are still pretty chaotic, and even when I'm at school, I can't stop thinking about . . . well, you know."

He couldn't know, though, or at least not completely. I wanted to take a knife and slash it through a really big canvas or throw red paint all over the stupid varsity jacket Trip was so proud of.

"Been there, done <u>that</u>," he said. "Before my mom moved away, I used to hate going home from school—in fact, in middle school, I hid in the library until the late bus came, just so I'd only have to spend an hour alone with her before my dad got there. I was actually glad when she was in the hospital because it meant things at home were less crazy."

I hadn't thought about this before, but he was absolutely right. Although I missed Cara when she was away, there was a peace in the house I appreciated. I winced a bit at the idea of being grateful to have someone in your family institutionalized and asked, "Will your mom ever come back?"

He played with the plastic stirrer from my drink, his eyes far away. "I hope not."

I couldn't imagine life without a mom and blurted out, "Don't you miss her—at least a little bit?"

He looked me right in the eyes. "No. In fact, I'm even more relieved now than when she used to go in the hospital because I knew eventually she would come home." He fiddled with his empty cup. "You don't know what it's like to have the one person who's supposed to love you unconditionally hate your guts . . . but that's over now."

161

He looked over my shoulder with one of those faces that you can just tell takes a lot of effort to put on. I was thinking maybe it wasn't really *over* for him, like he claims. After a few seconds, he seemed to realize I was still there and gave me this little smile. "Anyway, my dad is great, and when I go off to college, no one'll ever know anything about my past."

"Are you going pretty far away, then?" I asked in a small voice.

He smiled again, that dreamy sweet smile I adore. "London. I'll be able to travel all over the place from there. You should think about it, Megan. Think of all the great artists who came from Europe and all the good schools there."

What I thought about was my dad, standing in his pulpit every Sunday, doing that little tug on his collar that was a special signal to Cara and me about how much he loves us. For some reason, it was easier to imagine Mom and her welcome baskets carrying on without me than to picture him sitting in his study, maybe emailing me or, most certainly, praying for me.

Later, because Jeremy drives, I got to ride alone in a car with a boy for the first time ever. (Mom and Dad insisted on driving me there and spending a few minutes *getting to know* Jeremy, which actually went well enough that they allowed me to come home with him.)

He has this almost antique car with big wide seats and funny aquamarine panels that he only drives on *special occasions* because it takes so much gas. I was sort of flattered by that but a little uncomfortable until he turned on the radio so we could listen to music without having to worry about making conversation.

Watching the lights of the city slide by as I leaned back against the seat, I felt more relaxed than I had in a long time.

When we got to my house, he started walking me to the door, and I could just imagine Mrs. B with her binoculars across the street. (She might like me, but that doesn't mean she's stopped being nosey. Okay, I said to God, that was just mean. Maybe she really cares about what happens to me.)

Actually, that moment of guilt propelled me toward her house. "There's someone I want you to meet," I said, grabbing Jeremy's arm. (I already knew she never goes to bed before ten.)

Can you believe it was the most incredible time I ever had with her? She must have seen us coming, because she threw open the door without even pretending to be embarrassed about spying on us. Before Jeremy could say "no thanks," she swept us into the kitchen and sliced up a cheesecake she had made that afternoon, which was, of course, unbelievably delicious, even without globs of cherries on top like they do in restaurants.

Jeremy had two helpings, and then Mrs. B pulled out her art, which was what I dreaded most, since I know how long it can take her to *share* everything. (Oops, mean again. Must work on that.)

But Jeremy was really interested because he plans to visit Paris as often as he can, so for his sake, I sat through repeats of some stories I'd already heard two or three times. In the middle I went to the window of Mrs. B's living room and called Mom to tell her I wasn't breaking my curfew but was right across the street with Mrs. B, which made her peer out of our living-room window. I waved, and she waved back.

"Oh, Eggy, how nice of you. Take your time," she said, sounding a little surprised. Looking at her silhouette in the window from across the street, she seemed smaller and almost like a stranger— an anxious stranger. That made me realize how stressed she must be, worrying so much about Cara and her job and everything.

At 10:00 on the dot, Mrs. B was finished with us, so she sent Jeremy out the door with most of the leftover cheesecake and kissed my cheek.

"He's very sweet," she whispered in my ear, then yawned. "And I am very tired."

Not too tired to watch and see if he kisses me good-bye, I thought, but with a minimum of two sets of eyes trained on us, there was no way that would happen. At his car door, I gave him an awkward hug and said a quick *thanks.*

"You wouldn't believe how many people are watching us now to see if anything happens," I murmured, gesturing at the two houses.

"Well, then, let's give them something to watch." He laughed and swept me toward him in this big dramatic way. Then he took my hand and raised it to his lips and kissed it.

!!!
Posted 3/5 @ 11:55 PM

Congrats 6 Chats 3

Omg that is 2 romantik he is a keeper 4 sure. U must b in 7th heaven. Call me if u can—my sister just got admitted 2 a rehab nd I so need to talk to u!
Posted 3/6 @ 12:11 AM by zo4u

What a move! Look out, Mark—I might copy that one!
Posted at 3/6 @ 12:19 AM by kyleawhile

Bring it on!
Posted 3/6 @ 12:32 AM by zbest

CHAPTER 21

Wednesday, March 9

Boy, Zoey, we could write a book on being the sister of a sick girl, couldn't we? No one really understands what it's like until they go through it, although Maritza and Jess think they do.

"I know just how you feel," Jess said at lunch the other day. "Charlie embarrasses me all the time, and everyone is always asking me what's wrong with him."

Except she <u>doesn't</u> know just how I feel, because her brother is normal, pretty much, and didn't have something so terrible happen to him that made his family worry all the time. If it wasn't for the stuff about Mark, I would consider letting Jeremy post here, because I think he gets it, too.

Speaking of whom . . . Mom has decided it would be good for Cara to come along with us when we drive up to meet Mark on Monday, so I'm hoping a few hours in the car will give them an opportunity to have an honest conversation. Last night she invited me into her bedroom after supper so we could do homework together, another thing we haven't done in ages, since I don't need her help that often anymore.

"Cara, why don't you talk to Mom when we're driving?" I suggested. "That way she'll be distracted and have to look at the road, but you can let her know what's going on. I'll even pretend to be asleep."

She looked at me as if she was considering the idea, then shook her head. "No. If I can't tell my therapist, I can't tell Mom. She'll flip out."

"Your therapist is kind of weird."

She laughed and rolled her eyes. "You think? The other day she wanted me to pretend to be someone else in our house and act out how I would feel." For once, she dropped down on the floor, patted Casper, and then scratched behind his ears. "So I

pretended to be you, bad boy, always checking up on everyone and wanting to know what's going on."

"Did that help you in any way at all?" I added some pats of my own.

"Not really, but it was better than talking about my relationship with Mom, or how I supposedly feel about losing my real dad. I know it's sad, and sometimes I really do cry about it, but I don't see anything that big or emotionally significant about it—I was just a baby."

Then, Casper wriggled away, leaving us side by side on the floor. I lifted up my pant leg to scratch an itch (stupid me, there's still a scar from where I cut myself).

Cara leaned in closer, pulling up the cuff of my pants. "What is that?" she asked, pointing at the mark.

"It's nothing," I said, pushing the hem of my pants down.

But she knocked my hand away and pushed them back up, scrunching her face into a frown at the sight of the slash across my thigh. Frankly, I have regretted ever doing it about a hundred times, and one hundred and one occurred when I saw the shocked look on her face.

"Eggy, you cut yourself, didn't you?"

I acted like I was going to leave. "Just once, and it's no big deal. Believe me, I will be sorry forever if I have to keep explaining to everyone why I won't wear a bathing suit."

"It's because of me, isn't it?"

"No." She gave me one of her snotty hard looks, and I caved in. "Okay, yes, but not completely. It was just that Mom and Dad were so caught up in what was going on with you, they didn't even notice I was having a hard time. I was frustrated."

She touched the mark gently. "I'm so sorry. It looks like it hurt a lot."

"It did," I admitted, and at first it seemed like there was nothing else to say, but suddenly all these words were spilling out of me. "But believe me, I'm sorry, really sorry. It didn't make me feel better, either. Now I worry all the time that Mom or Dad or someone else is going to see the mark and get all bent out of shape. I didn't even go swimming in Arizona because of that."

"A lot of girls at the hospital were cutters, in addition to having eating disorders. I thought they were just doing it for attention, but now I think I might be wrong. Oh, Eggy, it makes me so depressed to think of you hurting yourself like that. Give me a hug."

I did, trying to reassure her that it was really no big deal and that she should be thinking about herself and the constant barfing she can't seem to stop and how important it is to tell Mom and Dad the truth.

"You must have been in the bathroom throwing up six times yesterday, Cara. It just about drives Mom nuts, and Dad goes into his study to pray every time he hears you going down the hallway. Why don't you try sitting down and talking to them?"

"Don't you think I would stop it if I could? If talking to Mom or Dad would make a difference, I already would have."

"But they don't know everything," I pressed.

"Eggy! You promised you wouldn't tell!"

"No, I didn't," I snapped. "I didn't promise a thing. I didn't <u>not</u> promise, either, but Cara, you could die from throwing up all the time—I read about it online."

"I'm not going to die," she scoffed, running her fingers through her hair, which looked scraggly and awful. It used to be her best feature, if it was possible for any one of them to be better than the others. Not eating right has ended that—along with her pimple-free complexion. Couldn't she see how she was destroying her body?

In the TV movie about the girl with <u>bulimia</u>, she dropped dead from heart problems because of a <u>potassium imbalance</u>. While I felt sorry and angry with Cara in equal measures, I wasn't sure how much more I could plead or argue or ask her to tell Mom or Dad or even her therapist about what Trip had done. At some point, it's going to have to come out.
Posted 3/9 @ 8:50 PM

Congrats 2 Chats 2

Heydah—u r rite! u or Cara need 2 tell—soon!
Posted 3/9 @ 8:56 PM by tennytrish

Hey grl, good luck on ur big date at the ski slope! U deserve a fun time nd lots of a1otion from both Jeremy nd Mark! Try 2 have a day without worrying abut Cara.
Posted 3/9 @ 9:01 PM by zbest

Saturday, March 19
Part One of the Long, Sad Story

So off we went to my big ski date, even though by the time the day rolled around I had already decided I have a serious crush on Jeremy (who went to Florida with his dad for spring break, most likely to see his mom). Still, there was a little bit of me that remembered how exciting it had been last summer with Mark, and being your basic romance-starved teenaged girl, I decided to go.

When we got to the ski lodge, Mark was every bit as cute as I remembered him. Even Cara gave me a thumbs-up behind his back when he came loping over to the entrance and gave me a formal hug (you know, the kind where your bodies don't touch).

"You look just like I remembered!" he said. Was that a good thing?

He looked <u>better</u> than I remembered: great black hair just a little too long (that's a tennis thing), eyelashes that look like they have mascara on them, and this totally buff body that shows what an athlete he is.

To give us some *time alone,* Mom and Cara quickly went off to shop at some outlets nearby, which would (hopefully) give Cara yet another chance to tell the truth. I watched them walk away, side by side with their shoulders almost touching, and prayed à la Dad that it would happen.

"So, which slope should we try first, or would you rather get something to eat?" Mark asked, reminding me of why I was really there.

If he knew I borrowed the ski gear I was wearing from Maritza and that I had to ask her why I would possibly need the same kind of snow pants I wore as a first grader to ski, he wouldn't have asked that question.

"How about hot chocolate?" I said, forestalling the moment when he would discover I was as inept at skiing as I was at tennis.

The lodge was crowded, mostly with teenagers, but Mark and I could have been all by ourselves on a desert island, since we only focused on each other. He had so many funny stories about learning to drive, his dog Bailey, and his school that I could have listened all afternoon.

Unfortunately, he seemed to get bored of the conversation pretty quickly, and nodded at the slopes, rubbing his hands together. "Shall we?"

I could tell there was only one answer, so I smiled and said, "Sure!"

A courageous person would have confessed that she had only skied once before in her life and used the money her mother had given her for a ski lesson without embarrassment. I was not that courageous person, though, so I followed after him like Casper does me, pretending I knew what to do.

It was easy to get through the boots part since he asked if I needed any help, and I laughed and pretended it was a joke to let him help clamp them on. I watched everyone else step on and off their skis and asked God to please make me be able to do the same thing when we got outside. There were little kids swooshing around in the snow—how hard could it be?

(An aside about God and why I prayed twice in such a short time: Dad and I had one of our long talks in his study last night, and I realized that while Mom is getting all charged up and energetic to help Cara, he is quietly carrying out his own campaign.

"I pray for her—and you—every night, but I've always done that. Now, I set aside two hours every day just to pray for her recovery." He looked so sad when he said it, I came over and sat on his lap and gave him a big hug.

"Why do you think God isn't making her better?"

"Eggy, you know things don't work that way, like a switch flipping. Still, I believe she will recover." He straightened up in his chair and patted my back. "This is a hard time for all of us, but we can't lose our faith over it."

Which made me wonder if I'm the weak link in the faith chain at our house. Sure, I go to church and all that, but ever since Cara got sick, Mom has been <u>more</u> religious, sometimes listening to Christian books on tape like <u>Becoming a Woman of Strength</u> [today] and <u>Your Call to Be a Mother of Courage</u> [last week]. She gets teary-eyed when she listens—are they really that helpful?

Dad would probably disown me if he read this, but if God can make Cara better, what's the delay? We're all struggling pretty bad here, and while He's at it, Jeremy seems like he could use some help, too. Am I negating all their prayers with my skepticism? That's why I decided I should try to talk to God as sincerely as possible.)

Anyway, there is a lot more about Mark but I'm kind of doped up on painkillers right now (which might explain the spiritual musings), so I will have to continue later. Ah, you might wonder, why is she on painkillers? Stay tuned. . . .
Posted 3/19 @ 11:15 AM

Congrats o Chats o

Saturday, March 19
Later . . . Part Two of the Long, Sad Story
Back to the ski slope.

"It's—ah—been a while since I actually got all geared up," I finally told Mark as we stood at the bottom of the lift. "Refresh my memory on how I get on these things?"

He wrinkled his forehead at me and gave me a quick demonstration. "You sure you're going to be okay, Meg?"

Ah yes, I loved it that he called me "Meg" since no one ever does. As "Meg," I could be a girl with a healthy sister, a bright and witty girl who would try anything, a girl who went to tennis camp and skied, even though she wasn't athletic at all. It was easy to bat him with the claw of my glove and assure him I was fine.

Given my fear of heights, the lift was terrifying, but I acted as if the cold was making me shiver and refused to look down. I tripped a little getting off, but Mark didn't seem to notice—he headed right for the hardest slope.

At least I took a stand after we got off the lift, pointing toward the green-rated slope, since I knew that meant "Easiest."

"I think I'll take a trial run down that one and meet you at the bottom," I said, watching him disappear with both relief and anxiety. How was I going to get to the bottom of the hill?

"Easy does it," I told myself, taking a deep breath. (That line always works on Casper when I'm about to brush him, which he hates.) Maritza had walked me through the basic moves, thrilled to be part of my romantic intrigue, and I'd watched dozens of videos online; all I had to do was use my weight to guide my skis.

I looked down the long steep slope of the hill, and my heart sounded like those rapid shoots Maritza does with her camera, taking about a hundred pictures really fast. I looked up at the overcast sky and said, "God, I can do this, right?"

Halfway down the slope, a person from behind me decided to pass by really fast on my right, which threw me off balance. Those instructional videos forgot to show what happens when something goes wrong and a person actually ends up cartwheeling on her skis. If a TV person had been there that day, I could have definitely provided the footage.

The next time I saw Mark, I was strapped in the rescue stretcher with a splint around my right ankle, which turned out to be broken.

"What the—?" He shook his head at me, confused, as if being brought down off the slope by the rescue team was a big joke I decided to play on him. Then, when the medics pushed him aside to load me onto the ambulance, he scowled.

"What's wrong with you? Why didn't you tell me you couldn't even make it down the bunny slope? Idiot!" He skied off before I could try to explain my false confidence.

"Nice guy," one of the female medics said, raising her eyebrows.

Unfortunately, I'll have <u>even more</u> on this later. . . .
Posted 3/19 @ 3:09 PM

Congrats o Chats o

Saturday, March 19
Still later . . . Part Three and End to the Long, Sad Story
As soon as the humiliation wore off, the physical pain started. Mom and Cara arrived at the hospital ER nearly hysterical, but I had been given enough morphine that I didn't care about anything except sleep. (Repeat of field hockey experience, only a bit worse pain and humiliation.)

After questions about whether I would need surgery or not, I ended up with a cast and crutches, a nice way to return to school after spring break, when everyone else is all tanned or relaxed. Cara was really sweet, though, and it seemed to help her to have something else to focus on other than her eating. She actually drove to the video store and got a bunch of old movies for us to watch on the last day of break, when Mom was at work and I was pretty much confined to the sofa or my bed.

Maybe it was my pain medicine or the joy of having Cara act normal that made me deliriously happy, but I found myself laughing at the movies harder than I did the first time through. Lisa's mom even drove her and Kyle over to cheer me up, and although I didn't think I could get any happier, they do this hilarious imitation of the teachers at their school that made me snort soda through my nose!

Later, Cara let me use her laptop so I could type while lying on the sofa, so that's how I'm able to write this, although it's taken me three installments, since I keep falling asleep. zzzzzzzz
Posted 3/19 @ 7:33 PM

Congrats o Chats 5

<sounds of shocked sympathy> Omg girl, u r lucky u dint hurt urself worse! We go 2 Colorado evry winter 2 ski nd it took me 4ever 2 learn—u were pretty brave 2 even try without a ski lesson—my ex BBF did just 2 show off. Neway, u shud think abut bing a writer becuz u can tell a story rilly well. As soon as I read it I had my sis drive me 2 the mall nd made u a *care package*—look 4 it soon! Luv u, <u>Meg</u>! (im gonna call u that now!)
Posted 3/19 @ 7:45 PM by zo4u

heydah, girlfriend, wut wud we do without u nd ur blog? Mebbe those girls at camp were rite abut him bing a player. My mom tellz me: *When something seems to be too good to be true, it probably is.* Wut will u tell Jeremy, tho?
Posted 3/19 @ 8:03 PM by tennytrish

Hey, you were pretty funny yourself today, skimeister. We should make a video and post it on <u>YouTube</u> as a *cautionary tale.* (Wasn't that what you called it?) It was fun to put stickers all over your cast.
Posted 3/19 @ 8:55 PM by kyleawhile

Mebbe itz a sign from God that u r meant 2 b /w Jeremy.
Posted 3/19 @ 9:02 PM by zbest

Jeremy <u>does</u> present a small problem, since I sort of told him I wasn't doing anything special during break . . . and I do hate to have any more secrets to keep track of than I already do. Maybe I'll say someone I knew from tennis camp called and asked me to go skiing, which <u>is</u> the truth, although it's not strictly the order in which things happened. See how tricky secrets get? It's just not worth it—but then there's the whole loyalty thing. I still haven't told my parents about Cara and Trip because I don't want to upset her. Anyway, off to bed for about the fourth time today—pain meds make you sleepy!
Posted 3/19 @ 9:27 PM by sistrsic92

CHAPTER 22

Sunday, March 20

Still incapacitated, bored beyond belief, and thinking perhaps I could find something to distract me, I was randomly cruising the web when I remembered that Mark told me at the ski lodge that he has a <u>blog</u>. I haven't heard from him since the Long, Sad Story, so I thought I would check it out. Bad idea.

First off, turns out he was sort of using me to make his ex-girlfriend jealous, and you should see the *picture* he posted and pretended was me! He talked about how sexy he *thought* I was and how he couldn't wait until after we were done skiing and cuddled up in the lodge. . . .

Next he wrote this totally sarcastic version of what happened, making me seem like the world's dumbest person (*dumb blonde* were his exact words, when I'm not even!). He must have taken a picture of the ambulance speeding away with his cellphone because that's how he ended the post. All his buddies commented on how totally hilarious the story was and how they agreed with his decision that I was an A+ idiot.

These kinds of things are like being on national television naked. Last year, just to be *funny,* Jess's brother Charlie posted a picture of a sexy model in her underwear with Maritza's face cropped on—you can imagine that was on for only about one hour before Maritza's parents were cursing him out in Spanish and demanding he remove it. Still, she said she got all these smutty posts on her blog and felt like a *puta*.

It took a long time for that to die down, as you can imagine, and it almost cost Jess her friendship with Maritza (don't think for a moment that yours truly became more sought after because of it; they both were mad at me for refusing to take sides—if anything, that's what made them forget about how mad they were at each other.) I can't imagine <u>ever</u> forgiving Mark!
Posted 3/20 @ 3:25 PM

Congrats 2 Chats 2

<sounds of angry growl> Dunt worry, check wut I posted on his blog—after all, even the EMT sed he wuzn't a very nice person. Who makes their date go off 2 the ER alone? I almost rote abut how a girl at camp tole me he cries when he loses a big match, but that seems 2 cruel. If you want me 2, I will.
Posted 3/20 @ 4:56 PM by zo4u

heydah. My rents are sending me to tennis camp 4 a week this summer—just wait until I see Mr. Playah! There will b balls bouncing, nd they mite not b the tennis kind. (Sorry, Megan, but

the loyalty thing means a lot 2 me, nd he hurt you, my VBF.)
neway—Zoey nd Meg, im goin to camp the 1st week—I hope u
do 2 so we can rilly show Mark U DON'T MESS WITH GRLFRENZ!
Posted 3/20 @ 5:30 PM by tennytrish

Monday, March 21

So, of course, I had to explain about a hundred times today what
I was doing skiing when in fact, if there's one thing I'm known for
throughout the school, it's my inability to do anything that
involves whole-body dexterity. Maritza is still mad about her ski
pants—by the time I got to the ER, my ankle had swelled so
much the nurse had to cut them off. My parents already gave her
the money to buy a new, nicer pair, but I guess she really liked the
old ones. I hope she won't tell everyone what really happened
because she's angry—I swore her and Jess to secrecy when I told
them the story.

Jeremy was the person I dreaded telling the most, but it was hard
to escape him. I was so conspicuous on my crutches he stopped
in the hallway right after homeroom, all concerned.

"Gosh, what happened to you?" he asked.

"I . . . uh . . . had a skiing accident."

He checked my face to see if I might be kidding, then narrowed
his eyes. "Since when do you ski?"

"Obviously, since never," I said, lifting my casted foot a bit and
giving a little laugh. It seemed wisest to avoid the whole topic of
why I even tried.

He looked like he was about to ask more questions but then just offered to carry my books to my class, which he did in silence. I wanted to tell him what really happened in case Jess leaked the story (with *embellishments*—Charlie isn't the only one in her family who does that), but if skiing is hard, maneuvering through crowds of kids on crutches is worse. I was concentrating so hard I couldn't think of anything to tell Jeremy that wouldn't also expose my true motives for going skiing.

By the time AAP rolled around, it was obvious he had heard something, since he didn't even say hi when I hobbled in. Mr. Walker helped me get my supplies out and cleared a bunch of desks so I could prop up my leg. The whole time, Jeremy kept his head down, working on his own sketch.

"You know, we're getting close to the competition, and you really need to buckle down and show you're serious about this, Megan," Mr. Walker told me, leafing through my portfolio. "Do you think you can finish up these two pieces by next week?"

I looked at the collection of collages glumly, thinking there was no more room for false confidence in my life. I had certainly caused myself plenty of problems because of it already. The photograph/drawing idea didn't work out as well as I had hoped, and the lace overlay didn't look that great, either. My best bet was the original stuff I had done, with my drawings and passages from books and random images of bizarre things, like broken chairs and ripped kites and thunderstorms at night, all mish-mashed together.

"I don't know," I said and, just like the idiot Mark says I am, I started to cry. The crying, of course, had nothing to do with the art competition or Mr. Walker and everything to do with my ankle and Mark and Jeremy and even Cara.

Like most teachers, Mr. Walker was completely derailed by my emotional outburst and petted my shoulder like I do to Casper. "I didn't mean to upset you," he said, looking around for tissues.

It was Jeremy who came over with a handkerchief he pulled out of his pocket and handed to me. (Who knew people actually carry those things around?)

"I . . . I . . . think I should go h-h-home," I managed to say, and to his credit, Jeremy offered to drive me. I had to call Mom and get an "okay" before that could happen, but at that moment, I would have walked/hobbled home if it meant getting out of there as soon as possible.

I pretty much had his handkerchief completely soaked halfway through the trip.

"I'm sorry to make you miss AAP," I said, sniffling and not daring to look at his face for fear of the expression I would see there. Here was a boy who had helped both me and my sister for no apparent reason, and what came of it?

"I'm pretty much finished, so I don't mind," he answered. There was a long silence, then I took a deep breath and spilled everything.

"Jeremy, my mom and Cara took me skiing so I could meet up with a guy I met at tennis camp last summer. I don't know what you heard, but that's the truth of it. I guess my life here is so sad,

I needed something different to distract me, but now I'm sure there are all kinds of rumors flying around."

I went on to tell him what happened—only slightly edited—and ended by describing Mark's blog post about me. Jeremy just kept staring at the road, shaking his head slightly. When we got to my house, he parked and helped me out of the car.

At the door, he paused for a second. "What I don't get is why you and your sister go after guys who are such jerks. From what I can tell, you have a pretty nice dad."

That *pretty nice dad* appeared at the door and took my stuff from Jeremy. He invited him in, but by then I think Jeremy had had a Megan overdose, so he mumbled an excuse about having to get going.

I struggled up the front steps after Dad as best I could with only one good foot and put my hand over the doorknob. Jeremy was right behind me with his arms out, like he expected me to slip and fall again.

"You're wrong," I told him. "Cara and me might <u>attract</u> jerks, but in my case, I fell for it because I didn't think anyone else would ever really like me."

"So why did you go out with me if you didn't think I liked you?"

"I went because I wanted to, but I guess I thought you were just being nice to me because you felt bad about what I was going through." I couldn't look at him when I said those words. In fact, I couldn't even believe I did say them and prayed Dad wasn't within hearing range.

Jeremy snorted. "A pity date? That's a new one."

I had to laugh. "Hey, can I help it if I have a major inferiority complex? You would too if you grew up with Cara." Then I realized I really didn't feel inferior to her anymore. "Well, the old Cara, anyway."

"As an only child, I wouldn't know about that, but I do know I'm not the kind of person to go out on a 'pity date.' I hope you feel better." He did the slow, sweet smile thing and bounced down the steps and back to his car.
Posted 3/21 @ 8:10 PM

Congrats 4 Chats 2

U r 2 honest 4 ur own good, girl! I wudnt have told ne1 wut rilly happened—I can see why u think that ur friends r just *sort-of*—why wud Jess tell a secret like that 2 the whole skool? Btw, did u see what Mark rote back 2 me on his blog? He sed my tennis is worse than ur skiing! What an ass. I'm sorry, but itz true.
Posted 3/21 @ 8:31 PM by tennytrish

It gets worse. Cara told me one of her friends said I was making out /w Mark and fell off the lift! If Jeremy heard that, I can see why he would wonder about me. I did tell her what he said about us picking loser guys when we had such a nice dad, and Cara said that's just not true, and that we would both be thrilled to find guys as nice as Dad if there were any at our school. We agreed Jeremy might be the only one. She said she was going to email him and tell him the kissing rumor was a lie . . . but if he heard it via Jess, he might not believe a girl's supposed friend would make up something so vicious.

Posted 3/21 @ 8:45 PM by sistrsic92

CHAPTER 23

Wednesday, March 23

Mr. Walker was so concerned about me he called Mom that night, but I told her he was known as a worrywart and an exaggerator.

"I just had a long day," I said, which was the truth.

She hovered by the foot of my bed. The calculating look I know well was on her face. (I see it whenever she's trying to figure out how much a house she's hoping to sell is worth.) I could tell she wanted to believe me but was also afraid she had another disturbed daughter on her hands.

Why couldn't she just sit down and rub my back like she used to when I was little? Then I'd spill <u>everything</u>.

"Are you sure?" she asked me for the umpteenth time.

"Yes, Mom, I'm sure." I faked a yawn. "I'm really tired."

Finally, she settled Casper in on the bed next to me and left, maybe not completely convinced I was okay, but not concerned enough to hang around and pepper me with questions, like she does with Cara. I heard her go next door and then the murmur of her and my sister's voices, which gradually grew louder.

Nothing new—they've been fighting a lot since Cara refuses to try keeping even a morsel of food in her stomach. This morning when I struggled down the steps, desperate for orange juice and toast, the kitchen was a mess from one of her binges: empty food containers everywhere, the sink full of dirty dishes, and no bread left for me to eat. Mom had both her hands on Cara's shoulders.

"Please stop this!" Mom's eyes were shiny with tears as she spoke.

I slumped down on the bottom step, guessing that there wasn't anything for me to eat, which distracted them both. Cara came over and got my crutches and helped me limp over to the table, and Mom disappeared in her room for a second and returned with a box of granola bars and a few bananas.

"It's pretty bad when I have to hide food so Eggy and Dad have something to eat," she said, plunking the teakettle on the stove. Cara went upstairs, as if the mess in the kitchen had nothing to do with her.

I more than hate eating dinner with Cara because I know she will immediately run upstairs and throw everything up. I start dreading it an hour before we actually sit down at the table. It's just awful. She doesn't even try to hide it, and my *suggestion* that Mom should try and talk to Cara's therapist wasn't received very well. "Megan, don't you think I've already called every doctor and clinic and therapist I can find? Am I such a shitty mother you think I don't even care?" Mom said, her voice all quivery at the end.

I don't think that at all. She and Dad <u>have</u> tried everything to distract Cara and make her better: trying to play cards after we eat, suggesting we watch a nonfood channel show on TV together or go for a car ride, and even one of them standing like a guard in front of the bathroom (which I can't help thinking of as the barfroom). I know Dad still prays about it constantly.

Sitting at the table this morning, it seemed we had reached about the worst part of Cara's illness, because we've gone through medication, special clinics, and therapy—and Cara is getting worse. I'm the only one who knows the one thing that will help her: telling the truth. But will she ever do it? Btw, the rumor at school about me and Mark has quickly been replaced by a rumor that Cara and Tonya are having a vicious word war over Trip. As if!
Posted 3/23 @ 9:10 PM

Congrats 2 Chats 3

U need 2 sa sumthin no matter wut ur sis axd! Itz not fair 4 her 2 xpect u 2 keep that secret
Posted 3/23 @ 9:34 PM by zo4u

I gree, xpescilly b/c if it wuz me, one of my sis's wud tell on me in a heart ♥
Posted 3/23 @ 9:55 PM by zbest

Maybe she could tell a teacher or sumone else she trusts? Even your neighbor? There must be someone she can talk to!
Posted 3/23 @ 10:17 PM by kyleawhile

Thursday, March 31

Today started so incredibly good it's hard to believe it could end so incredibly terrible. At lunch, Maritza told me that Jeremy has been watching me all the time at AAP when he thinks I'm not looking and assured me he has the hots for me, in spite of my crutches and cast and only being able to wear sweatpants every day. That gave me sudden status in Jess's eyes again, too, since having a junior interested in you is even better than a boyfriend your own age. (So far none of the guys on track she's targeted as potential BBFs have been interested, which has made her a lot less enthusiastic about running two miles every day after school.)

Sure enough, when Maritza and I got to AAP today, Jeremy was outside the classroom, waiting for me. Maritza kind of rolled her eyes behind his back in an *I told you so!* way and went inside without me. He held up two tickets.

"I know you're sort of incapacitated, but I also know you'd love to see this. Any chance I can wheel you around the museum this Saturday?" he asked. The ticket was to a <u>Frida Kahlo</u> exhibit that would only be in <u>New York City</u> for two weeks. He had sort of mentioned this when we had our last date, but I assumed the Mark fiasco would have made him invite someone else.

The idea of him wheeling me around in a wheelchair was too funny, but then I realized that's probably what would have to happen if we were going to cover any distance. I could make it from one end of the school to the other, but navigating an art museum was another issue.

"I'd love it!" I said, thinking of how great it would be to get away from Cara and all the problems at home, but then I wondered if my parents would let me go that far away with a boy, especially when I was injured. "But I'll have to ask."

When Dad picked me up after AAP, I brought up the idea right away. To my amazement, not only was he not bothered by it, he thought it might be an educational experience for me. (You can sell anything to your parents under the guise of education, I'm convinced.)

"I don't know . . ." Mom said when I announced the news at dinner. She still wasn't working full-time because of Cara's appointments with the therapist and the doctor, and she seemed irritable and not herself, or maybe that's just the general atmosphere at our house.

"It'll be fine," Dad said. "Jeremy seems like a responsible boy, and if he drives that boat of a car he has, she'll be safer than in the minivan."

Mom was staring at me with this unsure look on her face when Cara reached for the mashed potatoes. Mom grabbed her hand.

"Cara, you've had enough," she said, not adding what we all knew: my sister had no intention of actually keeping down the food she was now shoving in like a starved person.

"I'm hungry!" Cara shrieked, pulling her hand free and piling potatoes on her plate. With eyes of fury she smeared them with butter and salt and then gulped them down in big spoonfuls, glaring at Mom the whole time.

A minute later she was gone, feet pounding on the stairs toward the bathroom. The three of us sat there with our plates still full, too shocked to say anything.

I've never seen my dad cry—not even when the Kendrick baby died of cancer, which had everyone in the church weeping—but within seconds after Cara disappeared, tears rolled down his cheeks, slow at first, and then faster until he was shaking and sobbing. Mom went over to him right away and circled him with her arms, and they kind of clung to each other, which made me not sure what to do except lean over and pat his arm as best I could.

Cara just can't keep doing things like this, I thought, and suddenly, I knew what I had to do. I took a deep breath and picked up Casper for courage.

"I have to tell you two something," I said, and my voice must have sounded different, because they both looked up, puzzled—and worried, of course. They probably thought I was going to confess that I was bulimic, too. "There's something you need to know about Cara—actually about Cara and Trip."

I pulled out one of the chairs next to me. "Mom, you better sit down, too."
Posted 3/31 @ 8:17 PM

Congrats 2 Chats 2

<sounds of cheering> good 4 u!!!!!!
Posted 3/31 @ 10:05 PM by zo4u

U'll b glad u did it, but I bet things will b tuff the next few days. Hang in there!
Posted 3/31 @ 10:10 PM by zbest

Friday, April 1

The joy of Jeremy asking me out and being allowed to go was quickly overpowered by Cara's fury, when Mom and Dad confronted her with what I told them about Trip. I could hear every word of their conversation, and even though they were as kind and gentle as possible with her, she flipped out, saying she wouldn't talk to the police or anyone else. They begged and begged her, but Cara said if they did anything, she would lie and deny that it happened.

"Cara, why would you do such a thing? How could you lie and let him get away with it?" Mom asked.

"I went through hell once, I don't want to do it again. Everyone already thinks I'm super-jealous of Tonya—they'll say I made it all up to get Trip in trouble," she screamed at them, then dashed out of her room and pounded on my locked door. "How could you do this to me? I'll never tell you anything in confidence ever again, you brat!"

"Cara, Megan only did what she thought was best," Mom said. "Now, let's go downstairs and figure out a plan."

I knew Dad had already gone to call a police officer from our congregation (thin walls), but I didn't dare come out of my room to try and listen in on what happened next.

"You did the right thing," I kept telling myself, and judging from the look on Casper's face, he knew exactly what had happened and was completely on my side. Still, I felt really bad. If she hadn't been causing herself and our family so much hurt, I probably wouldn't have said anything, even though I never promised her I'd keep such a terrible secret.

Later, when I was just about asleep, a knock came on my door. It turned out to be Mom, with a mug of cocoa. Clearing away the stack of books on my desk, she set it down and gave me a forlorn smile, then rubbed my shoulder.

"That was very brave of you, Megan. Dad and I"—her voice broke for a moment—"are very glad you told us."

Mom said the police officer had come over and talked to Cara until she finally agreed to report Trip. Even though Cara didn't want to relive it all, she agreed she didn't want him to do the same thing to other girls and get away with it. "We have to take Cara down to the police station now," she finished, "so Mrs. B is coming over—don't worry, I told her you were probably asleep, so if you don't feel like talking to her, you don't have to. But someone will be here with you, in case we're gone a long time."

I struggled to sit up, not sure I wanted more information, but since there weren't any sounds of screaming or struggling downstairs, I thought it was safe to ask: "How's Cara?"

"She's okay. Resigned, I guess. When something like this happens, a lot of women feel ashamed and guilty." She paused, rubbed my shoulder again, and stared at the floor. "My best friend in high school was raped, and I had to help her through it. She ended up getting pregnant but never told anyone the truth about her baby's father."

"I'm glad that didn't happen to Cara, but I still hate Trip. I hope he gets in so much trouble for this. He—" I started to tell her about Jeremy getting beat up but then stopped, since I didn't want to drag anyone else into the situation. As it was, Jess was going to be mad, too, since I had told my parents that her brothers said Trip was bragging in the locker room about having sex with Cara. They might get dragged in to testify, for all I know.

"You're the best little Eggy a mom could ask for," she said, kissing me on the forehead. "And don't worry about being angry at Trip—even Dad isn't on the forgiveness bandwagon right now." She sighed. "You know, I sold them their house, and I remember how nice his mother was. She kept thanking me for everything I did—now I have to wonder what's really going on in their family."

And off they went to the police station, leaving me to be tucked in by Mrs. B. Actually, I didn't mind that much because she brought me a brownie and Casper a doggie treat. (He's such a traitor—ever since she watched him at Christmas he's forgotten all about the times she tried to shoo him out of her yard with her broom because he peed on the grass. He acts like he loves her as much as he does me. . . .)

Posted 4/1 @ 11:01 PM

Congrats 2 Chats 1

<hugs nd more hugs>
Posted 4/1 @ 11:10 PM by zo4u

Friday, April 15

After my confession, Mom and Dad switched Cara to another therapist, who suggested she start taking an antidepressant. This was traumatic for my parents but not a big deal at all for me or Cara (of course, she might be motivated by the side effect of weight loss). Tons of kids talk about whatever pills he or she is taking—Jess tells me Charlie is on three pills, two for his "learning problem" and one for depression, and lots of other kids take more than one medication for *mental health issues.*

After the police stuff got taken care of, Cara's new therapist suggested she start going to this outpatient program for girls with eating disorders. They'll help her with her schoolwork so she can stay up academically and graduate on time. It's about an hour away, and since Cara is in no shape to be driving, Mrs. B volunteered to pick her up in the afternoons. (I imagine those trips take only 45 minutes.)

Mom <u>had</u> to go back to work. Her boss finally gave her an ultimatum and since the outpatient program is incredibly expensive (along with Cara's private therapy and medication), she didn't have any choice. I noticed the welcome baskets aren't lined up in the back of her car, though, and she was really grouchy with Dad last night when he tried to massage her shoulders and ask if everything was okay.

My cast still isn't off, but at least the crutches are gone. At first I tried to creep around the house and avoid Cara, but gradually, she stopped acting like she hated me. (Maybe someday she'll actually admit I was right.)

I would never tell her this, but she has gained a few pounds and looks much better. At least you can see a resemblance to the person in her senior picture taken last summer—could it really be that long ago? This weekend she wants to drive herself to the mall, another semi-normal activity that gives me hope, although she wants to clothes shop alone. Who does that?

After a few days of back and forth, Trip got suspended from school. When the news first leaked, I was a bit of a celebrity, and Jess and Maritza had to fend off all the girls who wanted to sit at our lunch table and hear every last detail of what I knew. Of course, Trip's dad, Todd Senior, has hired an attorney who is suing the school for suspending Trip when the charges haven't been proven. Cara is going to have to testify against him at a hearing, and after that, everyone will know exactly what happened.

The girls at my school have divided into two camps: one that says they never liked Trip and thought he was a big bully, and the other that seems to think my sister somehow deserved what she got. The girls who smirk when they talk about Cara are the ones who really get to me.

Today, Jess was in the middle of describing (for the twentieth time) how Trip hit Jeremy in the locker room. Right behind her, two girls were whispering behind their hands and laughing while she talked.

"It's not funny!" I snarled at them so loud that there was this completely awkward moment of silence at all the tables around us.

I shoved my chair back and, as angrily as one can with a huge cast on her foot, I stomped off and dumped my tray. Of course, who should be at the cafeteria exit but Trip's crowd of friends, all staring at me with these evil looks but not saying anything. It made me wonder if they were just being loyal. But I really do think they knew Trip had done what my sister said.

I have to end on a happy note, though: I love Jeremy. I love, love, love him! Kyle and Lisa ended up coming along to New York City, and the four of us had so much fun. The art was incredible, but what impressed me more was how considerate Jeremy was about me having to move slow and stop all the time. (Even though Kyle thought it would be a hoot, I absolutely refused the wheelchair, since that would be just too weird.) One of the guards was nice, though, and let me use the elevator for handicapped people.

Kyle's dad had told him about a restaurant near the museum, so we got to eat food like Mrs. B makes, only better. Amazingly, some of the things she cooked for me were on the menu, so I wasn't totally clueless.

Lisa told me she thinks Jeremy and I act like we have known each other forever. We talked the whole way down in the car and the whole way back, mostly about good stuff, but for a little bit when we were taking a rest in the museum by ourselves, he admitted he does miss his mom sometimes, even if she wasn't a really good parent.

"Now my dad has a serious girlfriend," he told me, rolling his eyes. "She tries to pretend like she's going to be a mommy figure for me, and I hate it."

A little mental image of Mom with one of her welcome baskets appeared in my mind, and I appreciated her so much all of a sudden. For months I've missed her paying attention to me, but Jeremy really made me realize how lucky I am to have her at all.
Posted 4/15 @ 4:55 PM

Congrats 4 Chats 5

Wow, ur life culd b on tv or in the movies xcept I wud leave out Mrs. B since thaz just 2 much—how often duz a cranky old lady turn out 2 be rilly nice nd good-hearted? We think 1 of r neighbors poisoned r cat becuz he dint like her. Super congrats on Jeremy— u deserve sum1 like him. Do u think he's serious abut u?
Posted 4/15 @ 5:16 PM by tennytrish

Um hello, dear, he took her on a major date—of course he's serious! <cheering nd many hugz!>
Posted 4/15 @ 5:23 PM by zo4u

I meant duz J think Megan is his OTL bcuz /w my OTL that's how

it happened, nd we were 2gether 4 longer than ne couple at skool. In fact, he IM'd me the other night nd axd if I wanted to *hang out.* Not sure wtd. For me, my OTL will always be my OTL.
Posted 4/15 @ 5:30 PM by tennytrish

Thaz the problem /w blogging, you don't always know what the person is really trying to say unless they're just downright mean like Mark. I know you both are my VBF and wouldn't write anything to hurt me . . . and I wonder too . . . does Jeremy feel the same way I do?
Posted 4/15 @ 5:45 PM by sistrsic92

If you ask me, he does! Call it a guy thing, but all the signs are there.
Posted 4/15 @ 5:47 PM by kyleawhile

Monday, April 18

Dad amazes me. There was an article in the paper about what happened to Cara—no names were used, of course, but everyone knew who it was. That prompted a zillion calls from people in the congregation—sort of the adult equivalent of what happened to me at the lunch table. Dad told them he appreciated their concern and then said he couldn't discuss the details. Why didn't I think of that? It would have saved me getting all hot and bothered about Cara's reputation.

Cara is still at the outpatient program, but she and Mom decided that she could finish her semester in <u>Florida</u> with Grams. Either she'll go to a school down there, be homeschooled, or try an online program Mom found out about. She's so smart it doesn't really matter—she'll get all As anywhere (that part of her perfection hasn't changed). I asked if it would bother her not to see her friends anymore.

"What friends?" she said. "In case you haven't noticed, no one's really been calling or coming over to see me. My real friends are the girls at the outpatient program now."

I hadn't thought about it before, but it was true—the Cara from fall who <u>always</u> had friends over or was <u>always</u> going somewhere or doing something with friends had been replaced by the Cara who did nothing but lie on the sofa, with no friends outside of her family and perhaps (perish the thought) Mrs. B.

Speaking of Cara's former friends, Tonya is trashing Cara all over the place, and I suspect she's the one who wrote "Cara L. is a slut" on the bathroom wall at school. Who would guess Tonya was such a mean person underneath? (Anyway, Cara doesn't know about it, but Maritza was with me when I saw it, so you can rest assured the principal was there about five seconds later with the janitor.)

Grams is so much fun, I felt sort of jealous about Cara getting to live with her, even if it's only for a few months (she leaves in a couple weeks). Plus, Florida is way cooler than here, or at least the part near the beach where Grams lives—but Jeremy makes all that irrelevant. We talk or IM just about every night, and he drives me to and from school, which is way out of his way. If things weren't so bizarre at our house right now, I would ask him over, but what would we do—avoid Cara so she wouldn't be reminded of school and get upset? Talk to my mom about how great her sales are going, ignoring the fact that she's lost twenty pounds and gotten a lot more gray hair? Pray with Dad about his stupid board of elders, who are pressuring him to take time off?

Anyway, Mom already told me she wants me to stick close to Cara until she goes away, because we all need to support her, so that rules out weekends. At least I can still go over to Mrs. B's when I need to get away. Actually I've been sketching and working on my AAP projects over there sometimes. When I showed Mrs. B the pieces I'm going to put in my final portfolio, she acted really impressed. (Note the word "act." She could be trying to make me feel better, which at one time I would have thought was impossible, given her personality.)
Posted 4/18 @ 5:16 PM

Congrats 2 Chats 2

Don't worry, u will live happily eva after, I know. Look at me, Im still /w DB nd our group just made a demo tape that my dad promised 2 *shop around.* <gasps of awe & amazement> I think artistic boys r good OTLs bcuz they can express their feelings thru art or music. DB rote a song 4 me—I'll let u kno when we put it online.
Posted 4/18 @ 5:22 PM by zo4u

Mebbe . . . my ex OTL still won't tell me why he broke up /w me even tho we've started sort of dating again. I shud c if he wud switch from playing basketball 2 writing poetry, hehe
Posted 4/18 @ 5:30 PM by tennytrish

CHAPTER 25

Friday, April 22

I've been in a frenzy working on my final pieces for AAP. It was so hard to decide which ones to submit, and thinking about sending them away is killing me. (I do have pictures, but it's not the same.) I worked so long and hard on all of them, they were like . . . well Casper, almost. I love them so much, I can't stand for anyone to say anything critical.

Every day I look at them and sometimes add something or take something away, and I get a secret pleasure knowing they're mine. As of now, I plan to send in a collage based on a drawing of Maritza and Jess and another one of my dad. The one of M & J is built around a picture of them I drew surrounded by bits of things that make me happy: titles of movies we've watched together, pieces of photographs of each of them doing funny things, some other trivia, and then lace over top of the whole thing. Dad's has a religious theme, of course, but not in a traditional way, more symbolic, if that makes any sense. He really likes it and

says it gets first place in the art contest of his heart.
Posted 4/22 @ 7:56 PM

Congrats 4 Chats 0

Friday, April 29

I can't believe it. AAP is over. We all turned in our projects, and
Mr. Walker is going to send them off to the competition. At first I
was really bummed, both because I hadn't realized how many
new art techniques I tried this past year and also because it
meant my only real time with my OTL will be during car rides
to school.

Then Mr. Walker announced that he got a grant to create a mural,
and he wants all of the students who were in AAP to be part of it.
That means going downtown (such as we have here) on Saturdays
and painting the entire side of a building, along with the people
who live in the neighborhood. Better yet, Jeremy volunteered to
drive me, so I'll get even more alone time with him!

My cast finally came off today, and if you ever want to see something gross, look at skin that's been underneath plaster for a few
weeks, and there it is. The doctor told me my skin will get normal
pretty quickly, but he also said I need physical therapy to regain my
strength and coordination. Little does he know there wasn't much
there before my accident—but it is so much easier to walk now!
Posted 4/29 @ 10:29 PM

Congrats 0 Chats 0

Wednesday, May 4

So, since Cara's only in the outpatient program half-time, she was appointed to drive me to <u>Physical Therapy</u>, which I suspect is also part of a plot by Mom and Dad to heal our relationship, since Mrs. B would volunteer in a second. (Then again, maybe they saw her backing out of the driveway and knocking over her mailbox by accident the other day and think I'm safer with Cara.) Anyway, for the first time since I told about Trip, she actually talked to me.

"You know, I can tell you're jealous I get to go to Gram's, but believe me, it won't be a picnic. She has all those friends who come over and play bridge every day . . . how depressing is that? Besides, it's not for that long," she started out of nowhere, not looking my way.

"I'm not jealous . . . okay, well, maybe I am a little bit, but I understand."

"I'm not sure you do. After the hearing this week, there's no way I'm going back to school. I've been getting all these stupid emails from people I thought were my friends, and Tonya wrote some horrible stuff about me on her blog." She blinked as if there might be tears in her eyes, then brushed her hair back with one hand. "Some people have been really nice, though. By the way, I heard about what Jeremy did in the locker room. Were you ever going to tell me that, since you're so into sharing secrets?"

"I thought it would make you feel worse," I said in a quiet voice, then added a little louder, "No one told me the hearing is this week. As usual, I'm being left out of the loop."

She nodded. "It's tomorrow, but no one is deliberately excluding you. Mom and Dad just don't want to worry you. Anyway, this is just to determine if there's enough evidence to pursue the case, I guess." There was a little silence, but then she lifted her chin. "I'm sure Trip is spreading all kinds of rumors about me, too."

"You know how kids are. They'll forget about it soon. There's always the 'next big thing,'" I said. "Are you nervous about the hearing?"

We had reached the hospital by this point and found a spot right in front, so she held up one finger, signaling that she needed to concentrate on parallel parking, a skill I'm sure I will never master. Once we were situated, she turned off the engine and shifted in her seat to face me.

"Of course I'm nervous, but okay, I'll admit it: you made me realize it was absolutely the right thing to tell Mom and Dad about what Trip did to me. I wasn't thinking clearly—you know, when you don't eat, your brain starts to get some pretty jumbled messages."

I couldn't believe what I was hearing and checked to see if she had a joking look on her face. She didn't.

"When I talked about it in the outpatient program and with my new therapist, I started to get really mad that I ever let him get away with it. I mean, I was crying and everything right after, and he just kept kissing me and telling me how much he loved me and how it would be okay." She bit her lower lip for a second. "But you know how back in the fall I got all smart and gave Mrs. B a camera supposedly so she could spy on me and Trip?" I nodded. "That was just one of the ones I got from work when there was a sale at the end of summer. I used another one to take pictures of the bruises on my arms and legs from where he held me down and made sure the time stamp was on them. My attorney says they pretty much make the case. I also kept my ripped underpants, which don't really mean much, but it's one more piece of evidence."

"Wow. You were really smart."

"No, I was really dumb—dumb to ever think what he did was acceptable in any way. The first time he got rough with me, I should have walked away from the relationship. Don't ever let a guy do that to you, Megan."

As we went into the hospital, I told her about Mark's blog post, which wasn't anywhere near what she had gone through, but still an example of how a girl can fall for a guy because she thinks he's all that. She told me she thought Mark was cute at first, but clearly there was something wrong with him to act like he had.

"There's one more thing," she said, pulling me into a corner of the lobby and pointing at a chair. I sat down, and she sat across from me. "There's a secret of yours that I've kept."

At first I started to ask "What?" in kind of an indignant way, but then I realized I still haven't worn short shorts because of the ugly gash on my leg. That made me hang my head, because Cara could have told on me, too.

"Why didn't you tell?" I asked, my eyes fixed on my feet.

"Have you done it again?"

"No! I told you it hurt too much."

"So I guess I believed you, and I could see that your life wasn't as crazy as mine. I know you hide a lot inside, but you're funny and you're spunky and you deal with things better than I do."

Then she added, "You have to promise me you will never ever do it again, though, or I will tell."

I looked her in the eye. "What are you going to do—whip out a Bible now and make me swear like Mom used to do when we were kids and she wanted to guilt us into telling the truth?"

She gave a little laugh and shook her head. "No. I'll take your word."

"Okay, you've got it—and if you remember, I never promised not to tell anyone your secret, and I kept it private as long as I could."

She hugged me. "I know you did. You're a good sister."

So physical therapy was no big deal, except there was this way cute assistant who kept flirting with Cara while he showed me the exercises I needed to do. His name is Dan, and he's studying to be a Physical Therapist but working as an assistant in the meantime. He's really buff and athletic, and he kept coming back over to make sure I was *doing okay* (really checking out Cara).

"It'd be a great career for you if you like sports," he told her, and on the way home, I could tell she was still thinking about that, since the whole college issue is still up in the air.

"Dan's kind of cute, don't you think?" I asked as we pulled in our driveway.

"Kind of," she answered and smiled.
Posted 5/4 @ 10:45 PM

Congrats 2 Chats 1

C I tole u the 2 of u wud make up. It's time 4: Happily eva after. <contented sighs> Nd guess wut, the future world famUS band ther4u got itz first paying gig 4 this weekend!
Posted 5/4 @ 11:02 PM by zo4u

CHAPTER 26

Thursday, May 5

Trip is kicked out of school permanently for what he did to Cara. I guess her *evidence* was pretty convincing, even though until the end, Trip insisted she wanted to do it. She and Mom and Dad told me all the details over supper, not in a gloating way, but in the way people do when they can't believe something terrible has really happened to them, and they've survived.

"I was so proud of you, honey," Mom said to Cara, and Dad agreed.

I've noticed that Cara is still struggling with eating right, but when Mrs. B came over with a bag of doggie biscuits for Casper and this yummy apple tart, Cara actually took a few bites of it and said it was delicious. I wonder how Grams will cope with the whole eating thing, but compared to a few months ago, things are light-years better.

Posted 5/5 @ 8:17 PM

Congrats 2 Chats 1

Ur sistr is so brave! If u want u can tell her Kyle n me think she is gr8. call me if u think there's nething I can do.
Posted 5/5 @ 9:05 PM by zbest

Friday, May 6

Tomorrow Cara leaves for <u>Florida</u>, and although I was going to miss the mural painting to go to the airport with them, Cara insisted that wasn't necessary. I sat on her bed, watching her pack, and asked if she was sure she didn't mind me saying good-bye here at the house.

"I know you don't want to miss time with Jeremy," she teased, tossing clothes in the open suitcase, which was already overflowing. "I can tell how much you like him."

"I do really like him," I confessed. "But I still think it's pretty one-sided. He hasn't even really kissed me yet."

She raised her eyebrows like she didn't agree. "You know, I probably shouldn't tell you this, but Jeremy goes to the same therapist I do—the new one."

"You're kidding. How do you know?"

"His appointments are right after mine. We talk in the waiting room sometimes—but just for a few minutes." She paused, holding up a pair of jeans, then looked at me with narrowed eyes. "If you ever tell him that I told you this, I seriously will never speak to you again. Anyway, Jeremy's been having a hard time with his dad getting remarried. Give him some space, and see what happens." She held the jeans up to her waist. "Too bad we're not the same size—I'd let you have these. I bet Jeremy would really like them. . . ."

I grabbed the jeans and swatted her with them, then she bopped me with her pillow. Pretty soon Casper was running around in circles barking, and we both collapsed on the floor, laughing like crazy.

Next week the results of the art contest will be announced. I know I don't have a chance, but I'm excited for Jeremy since he is really good, and even Maritza might win something, I think. One of the things she submitted was a collection of pictures of her lunch tray every day. It was kind of funny, because sometimes me and Jess would put extra things on it, like a picture I drew, or a lipstick, or some of Jess's jewelry. I asked Maritza if it was supposed to be a commentary on the quality of school food, and she just gave me one of her killer looks.

"It's like life, Megan, you know? You start out every day with something new and different, and sometimes it looks pretty good and sometimes it doesn't, but you have to go through it anyway."

That was so profound, I had no comeback. When she looked through my portfolio, she didn't seem to get any kind of deep meaning from my pictures. Maybe I'm just not meant to be *deep.*
Posted 5/6 @ 6:56 PM

Congrats 2 Chats 3

Yeah, itz like music, sumtimes u can figure out wut it means nd sumtimes not. Hey guess wut—my dad has a business trip to New York City sumtime this summer, nd he sed I culd come along nd c u if itz okay /w ur rents. That wud be tolly kool—then I can meet Jeremy.
Posted 5/6 @ 7:10 PM by zo4u

Hoorah! I asked my parents, and they said it's fine with them—they'll even come pick you up and drive you to our house while your dad is working! Now tennytrish, if you could come, too, it would be great—like a real-time reunion. As you can appreciate, I decided tennis camp is not an option for me this summer—or any other. But I'm thinking of doing this art program Jeremy told me about, and Mr. Walker said he recommended me as a counselor for the art camp the elementary school is holding.
Posted 5/6 @ 7:30 PM by sistrsic92

I'm tolly going away 4 the whole summer—I signed up 4 this program where u travel around the country doing volunteer work—nd Kyle is coming 2! Call me nd I'll tell u evrythin.
Posted 5/6 @ 7:45 PM by zbest

Friday, May 13

Being the only child in the house opens you up to a whole lot of scrutiny you wouldn't get otherwise, but the good thing is Jeremy has started hanging out for a little while after he drives me home from school—under Dad's watchful eye, of course. (Having a parent who can work at home when he wants is a real liability sometimes.)

So today we found out that Jeremy got an honorable mention in the AAP contest, which is so incredible, since they had a record number of entries, and when we saw the first-, second-, and third-place winners, we were blown away by their work. Maritza and I didn't get anything other than the experience of entering a major competition, but the comments the judges wrote on both of our portfolios were encouraging. Mine said: "Innovative and thought-provoking!"

Mrs. B made a special dinner to celebrate for Jeremy—and I mean special. French people really do know how to take an ordinary meal and turn it into a party; we had flowers on the table and appetizers to begin with, then soup, salad, a fancy fish dish (which I could tell Dad was *politely* eating to be nice since he's more of a meat person). For dessert, of course, there was cheesecake, since she remembered Jeremy liked it. All this was eaten off her best china, which is really pretty—not that I'm into that kind of thing.

"My mother-in-law bought these dishes for me when I got married, and I still have every piece, fifty years later!" she told me proudly, holding one up so we could see how the light shone right through it. I thought of the dish Cara threw against the wall and wondered if Mrs. B didn't realize she was lucky in some way for not having kids. She also had candles everywhere and the kind of music you only hear on records and a phonograph.

The one downer to the night was Cara not being there, but she calls every day and seems to be doing really well—even Grams says so. She decided to do the online school, and she got a part-time job at a local souvenir store and volunteers at a nursing home, so I think she's pretty busy. She emailed and told me sometimes they let her help out in physical therapy with the old people, which she really likes. (Or maybe she's just hoping to connect with Dan when she gets back—I wonder if she'll ever have another boyfriend after what she went through? On the last day of my therapy, Dan gave me his phone number to give to Cara in case she has any questions about being a physical therapist, but I'm not sure if I should share it or not.)

This weekend we'll be finishing the mural, and then next weekend the mayor is going to officially present it in a ceremony. We ended up drawing this incredibly colorful group of people dancing, all different sizes and shapes, with the words: "Life is a dance, and everyone is your partner." The people in the neighborhood asked if we could clean up the lot right in front of the mural and make some kind of garden there so it looks really nice—that might be a summer project.
Posted 5/13 @ 8:55 PM

Congrats 3 Chats 1

Mebbe u n Jeremy will b famous artists nd me nd DB will b famous musicians—it can happen! I wish he culd come along 2 NYC this summer, but he's all into working at the local video store nd making money, plus he loves movies almost as much as music.
Posted 5/13 @ 9:23 PM by zo4u

Monday, May 16
BIG NEWS !!!
Jeremy asked me if I wanted to go to the prom with him—but in sort of an offhand way, like, "So, what do you think? You want to go to prom with me?"

216

Jess and Maritza couldn't believe *I* would be the one out of the three of us who gets invited to the prom for juniors and seniors. I told them I wasn't that hot about going because it seemed wrong, somehow.

"Are you completely crazy?" Jess asked.

"Cara should be there, not me," I explained. "It's her senior year and the last chance she'll have to go to her prom."

I was still thinking about that when Jeremy brought the subject up again, but he sounded sort of lukewarm. I said I wasn't sure because there were so many things going on in my life.

"Megan, sweetheart, these are memories you'll always cherish," Mom told me, when I asked her what she thought I should do. She has a scrapbook full of pictures of every one of her proms.

So I talked to Cara about it on the phone, and she said it was a good idea and told me to take lots of pictures so she could see what everyone looked like. Apparently she and Dan have been IMing, and I think I heard Mom discussing dating and driving privileges with Gram on the phone one night, so I wonder if she hasn't met some kids her age down there, too. She sent me a picture of her on the beach with Grams, and she's still way too thin, but she got highlights in her hair, which look pretty good.

Jeremy got an early acceptance to the art school in London, just like he wanted to, and that makes me both happy and sad. How will I ever see him if he's that far away, and what will happen to our relationship when he's surrounded by beautiful European women? He did suggest I might try to be an exchange student next year. I never really thought of that, but I got the application and might talk to Mom and Dad about it.

Jeremy's dad has an English accent, which is sort of cool. It turns out that's where he grew up, and some of his relatives still live there; but most of his adult life he's lived here. I've only met him a couple of times, when he's taken me and Jeremy out to dinner—one time with his girlfriend/almost fiancée, who is a little intense (she runs a catering business and has that sort of *sell* personality Mom does, only amped up about a thousand watts).

Oh, wow, I just got a phone call from Maritza, and she's agreed to go to the prom with Charlie, so we're going to double date. Poor Jess—I know she's gonna feel left out. Who would ever think Charlie could get his act together enough to be a semi-desirable boyfriend? He has, though—maybe it's the medication, or maybe he just *matured,* as Dad likes to say. He's even learning photography so he'll have something in common with Maritza (and not the kind of photography he thought was so funny on his website).
Posted 5/16 @ 8:10 PM

Congrats 6 Chats 5

Im glad u r going! Mebbe they'll have good music . . . nd hey, London izn't much farther away frm u than me! Neway, party hardy!
Posted 5/16 @ 8:30 PM by zo4u

heydah—London rocks! my prom did not. . . .
Posted 5/16 @ 8:36 PM by tennytrish

I agree—our prom wuz kind of lame, but when I wuz /w Kyle wearing a way kool dress nd getting a mani/pedi nd my hair fixed it wuz the best. He got me a gardenia bouquet—how cool is that? I can still smell it. I'll bring my pictures 2 church this week.
Posted 5/16 @ 8:45 PM by zbest

Hey even guys have fun, too. I never wore a tux before! Wouldn't want to do it every week, but it was a hoot for one night.
Posted 5/16 @ 8:57 PM by kyleawhile

Too bad you go to a different school, Lisa! We could have a prom triple date. Jeremy just agreed to double date with Maritza and Charlie, so I'm psyched!
Posted 5/16 @ 9:22 PM by sistrsic92

Thursday, May 19

Mom and I went shopping for a dress, which was really fun. It's been forever since she and I did something together that was silly and serious at the same time. I think she is the old Mom again, maybe because Cara is sort of out of sight and a bit out of mind, or maybe because she truly believes the bad times are over. We didn't find anything I really liked, but she says this weekend we'll drive to the city and see what we can find there. She even offered to take off on Saturday, which is a major selling day for her right now.

"Mom, it's not that big a deal," I told her, but she kissed my forehead and hugged me.

"I want to do something really special for you, Meg," she said.

Notice how no one calls me Eggy anymore? I guess everything that's happened has changed that, too, and I can't say I mind.

Jeremy has started calling me "Ganny," which is short for Meganny (what he used to call me) and that's special, especially since it sounds kind of different. Anything connected to Jeremy automatically goes to the top of the list of things I like.

After our shopping trip, I went over to Mrs. B's to retrieve Casper (now he likes to spend all day with her while I'm at school), and of course she asked if we were successful on our mission.

"Not really," I said, throwing the squeaky toy I had bought Casper and watching him chase it again and again, like little kids who have very high tolerance for repetition of things they find fun.

"One minute," Mrs. B said with this mysterious look on her face as she walked down the hall. That sometimes means she's made me a special snack, but today she gestured for me to come into her bedroom, a place I've never been before.

When I went in, not so sure of what was up, there were all these incredible dresses on the bed. There must have been at least twenty, all different colors and styles.

"From my party days in Paris," she said.

A year ago, if someone had told me I would one day be thrilled by Mrs. B's clothes, I would have bet some serious money against it. These dresses, though, were to die for! I mean, some weren't right for me, but two of them looked like the kind of outfits I just might be able to pull off. When I tried them on, she stood behind me and twisted my hair up with her hand so my shoulders were bare, and I couldn't believe how incredibly sophisticated I looked for a tenth grader. I could only imagine Dad's comments, but if he walked down the hallway of my school any day, he'd see lots of girls showing way more skin than I was for no special occasion.

The one I liked best was this sort of aqua chiffon three-quarter-length dress with spangles on the top that looks a bit old fashioned, but in a neat vintage kind of way. I called Mom and told her to come right over, and when she got there, she too was amazed by what I found in the secret shopping mall of Mrs. B's bedroom.

"It's perfect!" she said. "And it's one of a kind—I bet you'll be the only girl there with a dress that's been worn in Paris!" She nudged me and winked at Mrs. B, who felt really proud of herself for all this, I could tell. She said she didn't mind if Mom got some alterations to the dress, since the top was a tiny bit tight. Then she searched through her photo album until she found a picture of herself and her husband when she was wearing the dress, and if I can look half as beautiful on prom night as she did back then, I will be ecstatic. (It's also sort of grim to think what I might look like when I'm her age. . . .)
Posted 5/19 @ 4:44 PM

Congrats 4 Chats 1

There's nothing like finding the perfect dress, is there? nd u sound like me, the kind of person who wants sumthing different. we have a dance at the end of the year, 2. Me n DB have r outfits planned, we r both going punk rock /w a goth twist—I will post pics! mebbe Mrs. B has sumthing 4 me?
Posted 5/19 @ 4:59 PM by zo4u

Saturday, May 21

Cara is coming home next weekend, but just for long enough to see me in my prom dress and visit Mom and Dad. She's decided to stay in Florida for the summer, and Grams doesn't mind, so I guess I'll have to go down there if I want to see her. Maritza volunteered to come along, which I've decided I wouldn't mind that much, although Gram's little condo filled with teenaged girls might be a bit much.

Jess always spends the summer in Idaho helping on her aunt and uncle's farm, which makes me feel sorry for her. There is some good news for Jess, however—she got a date to prom, too. I think Charlie might have had something to do with it, but at least she'll be coming along, which has all of us so excited. We're going to have a sleepover at my house the night before, and Cara volunteered to play chauffeur the next day and drive us around to our hair and nail appointments.

Given everything that's happened this year, I guess Maritza and Jess have proven themselves to be true friends, although in a different way than my blog buds, of course. Maybe I'll start a new blog next year and let them post, too, so you can all get to know each other.

Posted 5/21 @ 8:10 PM

Congrats 2 Chats 0

Saturday, May 28

I didn't recognize the person who got off the plane today. Not only is Cara's weight close to what it used to be, but her face looks normal too—even happy. You could see it in her eyes, and from the absence of all the stress lines that used to be there. She has curves again and is tanned and more blonde than I've ever seen her. She looked truly gorgeous!

Mom and Dad both got teary-eyed when they hugged her, and then Grams, who was right behind Cara, told me I looked like I grew about five inches since she saw me at Thanksgiving. I couldn't wait until we got home so I could get the scoop on everything from Cara, but of course Mom followed her right upstairs and wouldn't stop talking to her and hugging her.

At lunch we all went out for Chinese, and for the first time in too many months to count, Cara just ordered along with the rest of us instead of taking twenty minutes to decide what she wanted. She picked at the food when it came, but she still ate half of it and didn't run to the bathroom afterward.

When Jeremy came over later, Cara was really nice to him. After he left, I took Cara up to my room and showed her the dress for prom. She said it was perfect.

"You're going to look beautiful, Meg," she said. "And Jeremy will be a great date, I know." She hugged me and flopped on the bed, enough for me to see a small heart tattoo on her right hip.

"Hey, is that what I think it is?" I asked, tugging at her pants.

"My therapist says it's not such a bad thing," she said, pulling them back in place a little too quickly. "He said focusing on my body in other ways can actually be good for me. But don't tell Mom or Dad—<u>I mean it</u>!"

I laughed and said I could promise that, then asked, "So how's the new therapist working out?"

"Really good—he's the first guy therapist I've had . . . and I think that's helped, at least a little. The very first time I saw him, I just came right out and told him what happened. He referred me to this support group for girls who've been sexually assaulted, and it turns out a couple of them have eating disorders, too."

I was scratching Casper's back, unsure whether I should ask what mattered most to me. I decided to try.

"Is it . . . how is. . . ." My voice trailed off.

"The bulimia?" she asked softly. "It's still there, some, but it's lots better. I don't know . . . being with Grams, and away from everyone at school, and now I have this totally awesome job and the volunteering at the nursing home . . . it's just given me a different way of looking at things. My therapist says I have a lot of work to do, but that's why I want to stay in Florida and come back here in the fall. The community college has classes I can take to start my PT degree, until I decide where I want to go."

"Won't you miss Mom and Dad, though?"

"Of course—I will! I do already, but they're going to come down, and you better, too." She hugged me. "Mom said maybe I could even find a swim camp for you or something, this summer."

"Oh, please!" I rolled my eyes. "I think I've proven once and for all that I don't have an ounce of athletic ability."

She nudged me. "Just kidding. Anyway, I imagine you want to spend as much time as possible with Jeremy, right?"

"I hope so!" I said. "But I don't know what I'll do when he goes off to London for school next year."

My face must have looked kind of down then, because she leaned over and ruffled my hair. "Meg—it's prom weekend! Forget about the future and have a blast! After this year, you deserve it. Now let me see what makeup you have, so we can decide whether to go shopping or not—and what time are Maritza and Jess coming over?"

She jumped up and started rummaging through my makeup bag (an old reject of Mom's), which made Casper too excited. While she dabbed eye shadow on and twisted my hair one way and then the other, he started running around and barking nonstop. As for me—I just sat there smiling and didn't even care that a new, improved version of the old Cara was telling me what to do.

I had my sister back, and she was absolutely perfect.
Posted 5/28 @ 2:00 PM